About the Author

Barrie was born in Bournemouth, and had theatrical leanings at an early age. After National Service he came to London and trained at several theatres and tours. His first play 'Teddy Boy' toured in the fifties and his own coffee house was opened in 1960 at The Seven Dials in Soho. It became famous, and infamous, for the many characters it attracted. Amongst its many customers were Quentin Crisp, Simon and Garfunkel, Paul Simon, Lindsey Kemp, Wayne Sleep and many, many more! From 1972 he became well known as a theatrical agent as well as presenting many children's musicals on tour. He also presented star concerts such as The Jessie Matthews Show at the Shaftsbury Theatre in the West End and Jim Bailey at The London Palladium. He has presented over fifty concerts with John Hanson, Frankie Howerd, Bob Monkhouse and many others. Lately he has toured his one man show and numerous 'Songbooks', mostly 'West End to Broadway', 'The Cole Porter Story', and others. He has written children's musicals which have toured the UK and had his own gossip column in the late 'Plays and Players' magazine. He recently had his first novel published and is writing more projects. At the age of eighty-five he looks back over the years and tries to recapture the many excitements, victories and memories he has enjoyed.

Barrie Stacey

A TICKET TO PASSION

AUSTIN MACAULEY
PUBLISHERS LTD.

A CIP catalogue record for this title is available from the British Library.

ISBN 9781786292285 (Paperback)
ISBN 9781786292292 (Hardback)
ISBN 9781786292308 (E-Book)
www.austinmacauley.com

First Published (2016)
Austin Macauley Publishers Ltd.
25 Canada Square
Canary Wharf
London
E14 5LQ

Chapter 1

In the misty, grey of a November day, Emma saw her mother, Rose leave this world. It was three o'clock precisely and she was gone. Her sunken cheeks told of the pain and anguish she had endured these past eight months. Emma drew the pink sheets around her mother's head as if to try, at least, to provide some colour to the sombre scene. She shed tears and they kept coming although she tried her utmost to restrain them. Not that the death of her mother was a shock, far from it. She and her brother Teddy had known that it was inevitable for months. Cancer is a frightening creature, not caring who it blights. Perhaps Rose Jones had known it, but one would never have known.

Emma sat with her mother for a while and then slowly and lovingly, patted the pink covers and drew the sheet over her mother's sad frame and that was that. Emma stood up and looked out of the window, down on the carefully tended garden, the tall trees bordering the flower beds where many flowers had grown over the summer months, just as her mother intended. Rose had loved her garden and the garden had loved her. Who would look after it now?

So many questions invaded Emma's mind, and she felt so alone. Emma and her mother had been inseparable; one guarded the other, the old and the very young. Her mother had been her world, her life, her very

9

being. Oh, there was her brother Teddy of course, not that she saw much of him. Teddy was cock of the walk.

If looks mattered, he had the lot.

Emma started reminiscing. She recalled the trips to the market, the trips to the seaside where on one occasion, they even went fishing. A fisherman had showed them how to prepare their lines. His name had been Joey. It all came rushing back and it all belonged to Rose, her mother, who was no longer in her world and had moved on to the next. Emma's father, Fred, had been killed in a car accident when she was very small so her recollections of her Dad were distant and obscure.

Now, all she had was Teddy, and he really didn't have time to bother with her. She supposed that he was really very good looking now she thought about it. He had broad shoulders, a six pack, and was all of six foot tall, with a very masculine face, blonde hair and blue eyes that twinkled when he smiled.

Then there was Aunt Clara, her mother's sister. There was no mucking about with her! She would be down from her Yorkshire home as soon as she knew and would see to everything. Teddy didn't seem to get upset, like Emma. He hadn't grown up at home, being away at school and then at college. It was only when he was twenty-one that he came on the scene. He never remembered birthdays and the presents that he produced at Christmas were minimal. Emma pursed her lips and her brow was furrowed. She had to admit that she didn't know her brother much at all. When he left college, Teddy had seen that a local gym was advertising for staff. Teddy thought it might be a good idea, and help with his already toned appearance. He applied and the manager eventually gave him the job.

"You help out and you make sure that all the equipment is safe and working properly. I will be keeping an eye on you!" the manager said sternly.

All seemed to be going well, and Teddy enjoyed the job as well as doing regular work outs himself. Then Kate, an Olympic hopeful, started at the gym.

Teddy noticed her immediately. She was often there with her father who was a wealthy financier. He adored his daughter and indeed was her coach. He loved being involved with any of the national press that accompanied his daughter, for after all, Kate was to represent the UK. The gym was busy and Teddy, who was more 'eye candy' than anything else, became careless. He waltzed about flirting with the women and, some of the men, and enjoyed the attention he was getting. He neglected the mundane tasks, didn't check things through too thoroughly and then the accident happened; a large piece of equipment collapsed and with it Kate Ransom. The piece snapped in half, like a chocolate biscuit, and she was fatally wounded. Her father was devastated. Teddy was immediately sacked, the gym was sued for malpractice and forced to close. There was another gym in the town and Teddy tried to get a job there, to no avail. So Teddy idled his days away just hanging out, and getting into mischief.

Much of Emma's education had been missed. Oh, she knew there was something called sex that produced the next generation and that it happened between a man and a woman. Much of life confused her.

She realised that she was backward, but somehow she managed. She hadn't given the subject of sex much thought and Rose hadn't really got round to discussing the facts of life with Emma Mrs. Alice Blake, a neighbour, rang the doorbell. It screamed to be answered and Emma went downstairs to see who it was.

"Is Rose better?" enquired Alice Blake, who was a kindly soul.

Again Emma couldn't quite control her tears, but she wiped them away bravely, and gradually she told Alice that her mother had left them. Alice rushed upstairs and said farewell to the woman she had known for many years. She kissed her tenderly on the forehead, and arranged the covers neatly.

"Where's Teddy?" asked Alice.

"I really don't know," Emma shrugged. "Possibly at a football match or gambling."

"I might have known."

Alice made Emma a cup of very strong tea and sat down next to her on the sofa.

"You'll have to ring your Aunt Clara, Emma. She must be told at once. She will see to everything, she's much more organised than Teddy. He wouldn't have a clue how to go about things. Now do have a biscuit, Emma, biscuits go so well with a cup of tea."

Emma went to the sideboard and brought out the biscuit tin.

"Thank you," Alice smiled. "Now, Emma, things won't be easy for you but, in time, your life will change and you will find that you have grown up. Your childhood will be gone and you won't be sixteen for much longer. Time is consuming and the memory of your mother will linger in the background while you get on with your life. You can take my word on that."

An hour later, Teddy eventually came home and Emma told him the news.

"It had to happen Emma, we both knew that," he said. "Where do we go from here?"

He climbed the stairs to his mother's bedroom and stayed for a short while. He had been the apple of his mother's eye. She had adored him and had spoilt him rotten.

"I think it's time for a drink," he declared when he came downstairs.

"You could be right," said Alice. "It will help soften the blow. I know that all this is so sudden, but life is often like that. Look at the way my cousin Albert went. Here today and gone tomorrow."

Teddy looked at Alice and then at Emma. "We'll have to ring Aunt Clara," he declared.

"All done," said Alice. "She'll be here at ten o'clock tomorrow, and when she says ten o'clock, she means ten o'clock." She gave Teddy a sharp look. Teddy brought out the whisky bottle and the three of them raised a glass.

***

Clara Sullivan arrived the very next morning. A tall imposing lady of sixty-seven, she had been very close to her sister, Rose, and had often come down and stayed for a few days. She liked Emma and had tried to instil a little ambition into Teddy, usually to no avail. "Leave everything to me, you two," Aunt Clara ordered. "I know what I have to do, and I will do it."

As good as her word, Aunt Clara arranged the funeral. The three dozen friends attended, and she arranged refreshments in a nearby hotel.

The vicar was adequate and she chose the hymns carefully, even including a couple of well-loved ditties that Rose had liked. The whole affair ended very satisfactorily and she knew that she had done a good job.

Teddy was bland, as he was most of the time. Emma had cried a little, but Alice had put her arms around her and softened her sorrow.

Teddy ventured what was to become of them.

"I know what your mother has willed," announced Clara.

Teddy looked at her. "Yes, I thought you would."

"You both inherit the house and all in it, but I am afraid there is very little money."

Emma suddenly spoke. "How will we live?"

"Your mother, Emma, has instructed her solicitor to give you two hundred pounds a month from the estate to make sure there is always food on the table. Teddy, she has left you a lump sum of five thousand which you are not to fritter away!"

Aunt Clara looked at Teddy. "You, Teddy, will have to get a job. In my opinion you should have done so long ago, but it wasn't my business. I wouldn't dream of interfering."

Teddy looked at her sharply "No! Of course not!"

He lit a cigarette and shrugged his shoulders.

Later, in his bedroom, Teddy surveyed himself in the mirror. Not bad, he thought. He knew he was the cat's whiskers and inwardly was delighted. Five thousand! He could have a good time with that!

At college, he quickly gathered the young female students' attention. He enjoyed sex and, one night in the dormitory away at college, he had seduced a willing lad and after pleasuring the boy and having tasted the water himself, he found it all pleasing and enjoyable. He just liked sex!

Teddy was now several years older and he preferred to service girls of all ages, creeds and types. After all,

God had given him a strong advantage and he was not going to waste it. He had noticed the blonde in the supermarket, almost before she had noticed him.

Young, very slim, and with breasts to die for. She was, he thought, a virgin to be initiated, explored and broken in. Her name was Fay.

He had bought products that he had no use for, just so that he could join the queue and look into her eyes, which were hazel.

Fay began to notice Teddy, or rather to acknowledge he had much to offer. His tight trousers did much to advertise his wares.

"Back again?" Fay remarked.

"I'm afraid so. I keep forgetting shopping I should remember."

"Why don't you keep a shopping list?"

"What a good idea!"

Fay smiled. "It does make sense if you think about it."

"I could have other things on my mind."

"Oh!" Her beautiful eyes became questioning.

"Perhaps I could meet you after work for a drink?"

"I could meet you on Friday, if that's ok," Fay suggested.

"What time will that be?"

"Eight o'clock." Her smile exceeded all expectations, her lips with just a smattering of lipstick, opened to reveal perfect white teeth. Teddy's blood began racing. This was going better than expected.

"Where do you live?" he asked.

"At the top of the town, near the heath."

"Then we'll have a drink at the 'Lonely Duck' and then I could take you home," Teddy said. "That's if you fancy the idea."

"A gin and tonic at the Lonely Duck could be irresistible," Fay murmured.

"Oh, Christ!" Teddy said to himself. This couldn't be proceeding better. The girl had personality and perhaps a little wit. It would all help when he pulled her knickers down.

"It's a date?" he ventured.

"Yes, it's a date!"

"I'm so glad," said the old bag waiting in the queue. "It's a good thing you weren't proposing or we would have been here all night!"

Teddy winked at the silly old bag. She wouldn't have had a bit of the other since the Great War! With a smile, he left.

"The very idea!" she said and moved up the queue with her shopping.

Friday seemed an age in coming. At last it arrived and, at 8.20pm, so did Fay. Out of her supermarket overalls she was indeed a dish, Teddy thought; a checked blouse and a black skirt with a top coat to match.

"We can catch the seventy-two bus. There's plenty about," she said.

"Oh, ok, then."

"I don't even know your name!" Fay said coyly.

"That's because I didn't tell you. It's Teddy."

"Mine's Fay."

"I know that. I saw your name badge in the supermarket," Teddy smiled and, for Fay, the heavens opened.

The seventy-two bus arrived. The evening was dark and as the bus proceeded a little out of the town, the road narrowed and was less populated.

"My house is on the other side of the heath," said Fay. She let her eyes wander over his tall frame noting, as she did so, his tight buttocks and the generous frontage that his trousers boasted.

"I told mother that I would be late," she said.

"I like a caring daughter," Teddy squeezed her hand.

The bus drew alongside the heath.

"This is where we get out. The 'Lonely Duck' is just on the other side of the road. You must have noticed it time and time again," she chattered.

"Yes, I think I have." Teddy helped her down from the bus.

"There's a short path to the right. It's a short cut," said Fay.

"I see you know your way around." Teddy noted with satisfaction that no other passengers got off the bus. The area did seem a little bleak. Just the right place for the some fun, Teddy thought. The night was dark and a little misty, but it wasn't chilly. He took her hand and led her along the path. He put his arms around her and gently worked his way so that his fingers fondled her small but appealing breasts.

"It really is a nice night," said Fay, relishing his fast attention.

"Let's sit down for a minute," suggested Teddy. "I mean – we hardly know each other."

"Well, alright." Fay got a little nervous. He certainly was a fast worker.

They sat on top of the heath and, he had quickly taken off his thick sweater.

"It's a lovely evening, why don't you take off your coat?" he suggested.

"I think I will."

A few moments later he was kissing her; his tongue pleasuring the inside of her mouth.

"I don't think I should be doing this," said Fay as she looked at his face which was full of promised delight. After another rapturous kiss, his fingers started to explore further and, in no time at all, her skirt was abandoned and her knickers slid effortlessly down her legs.

In a flash, his trousers were off and his generous penis started its journey. She accepted it with delight as if she had been waiting for it all day, all month, possibly all year.

"Do you have rubbers?" she asked.

"Oh, I don't need them."

Teddy was now pounding away and Fay crinkled up her face with pleasure. Then suddenly, they heard sounds of someone approaching, so he quickened up and delivered the goods. The footsteps receded and the strangers trod a different path.

"Was that good for you?" Teddy asked.

"I think it was. I'll have to have a wash before my mother gets hold of me."

Teddy was delighted with his performance, his body had responded beautifully and he knew that he was more than just hot stuff in the pastime known as sexual intercourse.

Fay gathered her skirt as fast as he buttoned his trousers.

"I don't think I want a gin and tonic at the Lonely Duck now, if you don't mind," she said.

Teddy didn't mind at all. It saved him a tenner.

"I'll see you to your door," he offered.

"You'd better drop me at the corner...." she began.

"Oh?"

"Well, there is my mother you see…"

He did see! The last thing Teddy wanted was to meet her mother.

"I understand," said Teddy. "Can I see you again?"

"Yes, please."

Teddy dropped her at the corner and she swept up her mother's drive, put her key in the lock and disappeared inside the house. Teddy smiled.

It had turned out to be a field day and he was more than pleased with himself and Fay.

***

Teddy was really not all that concerned that his mother had left them. She had always been a soft touch when he ran out of cash, which he did regularly due to his visits to the casino and his passion for the turf. He had a great fondness for gambling and several other vices. Teddy had always spent more than his father left him. Betting could be a mug's game, but its magnetism was fatal.

Let's face it, he reasoned, it was a lot of fun.

The town had only recently opened a new casino where the roll of the dice was an instant attraction. He was popular in the large town and his tender age and muscularly, toned build had not gone unnoticed by the young women who came his way. The added attraction of his striking eyes with a hint of danger was not a bad thing. He secretly thought that women were to be used, de-flowered and then thrown away. That he had lost his virginity to a member of the male species in that little interlude at the college, added spice to the pudding.

Aunt Clara had been down and re-organised the house, not always to Teddy's satisfaction. Clara was a

19

tall, angular woman with a rather sharp nose. She had married well. Her husband, Cyril, was a builder, and a good one. He was a jovial man, not handsome, but then not plain either. Money was no problem, their home was spacious and their bank account most agreeable. She was a regular at the local church and at one time, had sung in the choir. She called a spade a spade even when it was a shovel. She secretly felt that her sister, Rose, had married beneath her. Having no children of her own, Clara had always had a soft spot for Emma, but what she thought of Teddy was not recorded. At least Rose had given him a good education. Emma was not, in her opinion, very bright. She definitely was not the sharpest knife in the box; a strange and fragile creature and difficult to understand. Rose knew and understood her and had really protected her from life. Clara acknowledged her family duties and Rose had always treasured and admired her. Now, as head of the family, she repeated herself again.

"What do you propose to do, Teddy? College and education has been and gone and you now have to make a living and look after Emma."

"Yes, Aunt Clara, I have plans," Teddy looked confident.

"Plans, my dear boy, are one thing. Actuality and a wage are another. Don't forget Emma's pocket money has to increase. A young woman's necessities multiply as she gets older. Men never understand these things – or pretend they don't. Your poor mother didn't have much help when your father died. He should have made much better provision for my sister and that's a fact!"

"Emma will soon be of marriageable age and who knows who she might ensnare," Teddy declared.

His tone did not please Clara one bit.

"Sometimes, Teddy, you amaze me with your thoughts, that you do! What the Good Lord would say is another matter." Her fingers flicked the mantelpiece. "Dust again!" she exclaimed in disgust. "I don't know where it comes from! Of course I have offered to take Emma home with me for a few weeks, but she will have none of it. So it is up to you, Teddy, to tend to your sister, and make sure she has everything that she needs. Art seems to be her hobby and I must say some of her drawings are commendable. Whether they mature into a living is another matter!"

Teddy lit a cigarette and Aunt Clara frowned irritably.

"Teddy, smoking is not a pastime I favour. You should do it outside. You should also request permission to smoke in the presence of a lady, remember that!"

Teddy smiled. "Aunt Clara, I memorise every word of your advice. I think Uncle Cyril has to be congratulated to have obeyed your every wish for so long."

"Are you aiming to be rude, Teddy?" Aunt Clara glared suspiciously at him. "I do not tolerate such behaviour as you know."

"I heed your every word, Aunt Clara," Teddy smirked.

"If only you did!" snapped Aunt Clara. "Well, I have to go home tomorrow. I told Emma that I expect the house to be kept immaculate and in good order and you had better see that it is."

"End of lecture?" remarked Teddy insolently.

Clara snorted. "The very idea!"

***

After his interlude with Fay on the heath, Teddy thought the idea of a well-off older lady wasn't a bad thought. He could become a gigolo! There are always so many frustrated women seeking sex, especially from such a handsome well-endowed man such as Teddy. He reasoned that such creatures neglected by their husbands would be delighted with such a diversion.

After Clara's departure, there was the question of Emma. The question was, what to do with her? If only he knew the answer. However, he did have an idea.

At breakfast several days later, Teddy mentioned to Emma, firstly about the household bills and then how Emma could possibly help.

Teddy paused and coughed nervously, rather contemplating a river he didn't know if he should cross. Emma wondered what was coming.

"Emma, have you thought much about sex?" he asked. "You know, the mating of a man and a woman."

"Not really," said Emma. "I'd rather read a book."

"Not good for a healthy young girl like yourself," Teddy replied. "Sex isn't a bad thing, especially when it's done in moderation. I think you'd rather enjoy it!"

Emma looked at him coyly, not sure what he was suggesting.

"As you know, Emma, I've got a lot of friends and some of them really fancy you. They'd pay well for your company."

Emma smiled. Her brother did get some strange ideas. "I don't know what you have in mind, Teddy, but anything to help. I realise that we need help with pennies."

"It isn't normal for a young woman like you, Emma, not to experience the wonders of sex," declared Teddy.

"It isn't dirty. It's natural and can be fun! Why, you might even fall for one of my friends."

Emma paused to think.

"I don't know, Teddy. I really don't. Mother never mentioned things like that."

Teddy took her hand. "I know, but a little investigation cannot do any harm. I know you'll love my friend, Sam. I've come to know him well and he's in advertising, I think. He could be a little up your street, and besides that, he's good looking."

"Oh, well, if you think it will make me more worldly wise. I suppose girls my age are much more experienced in these things."

"Good," Teddy was pleased. "All my friends are really great guys."

"More toast, Teddy?"

"No thanks, Emma. I'm meeting a new girl today. She's been pestering me for a date."

Emma squeezed his hand. She adored her brother even if she didn't always understand him.

***

For a few days, Teddy didn't broach the subject of sex again. After all, the papers screamed of nothing else and Emma must think that it was a normal part of living. It was a rainy morning and the doorbell rang long and sharply.

Emma had gone out shopping. Teddy hadn't been up long and was still in his dressing gown.

"All right, all right," he muttered. "I'm coming, I'm coming!"

He opened the door slowly and there stood a woman of about forty-five.

23

She was smart, wearing a trouser suit and colourful blouse. Her make-up was perfect, and her blonde hair tumbled around her shoulders.

"I'm not expecting anyone," Teddy began.

"I've a hefty bone to pick with you, young man." Before Teddy could close the door, the woman had one foot inside.

"I don't know you…"

"No, but you soon will," the woman snapped. "I hear you've seduced my daughter. I think the word is rape!"

"I don't know your daughter and I don't know you," Teddy said coldly.

"I think it's goodbye, Madam."

"Not at all!" the woman replied. "I'm Fay's mother. You admit you know Fay?"

"Yes, she's the girl in Sainsbury's I think. I shop there sometimes."

"And pick up a quick fuck when you can," the woman glared at him.

"Really, Mrs. Who-ever-you-are," Teddy muttered angrily. "How dare you come here with your malicious lies! I don't know you, I don't want to know you, and my advice to you is to fuck off!"

"I know your sort," the woman would not budge. "I've been around you know."

"That, I wouldn't doubt!" Teddy gave her a wicked smile.

"My daughter came home in a shocking state, bruised and scratches everywhere," she stated.

Teddy didn't quite know how to handle this. Should he lie, deny the whole situation or go along with it? After all, Fay had put up no resistance, so it couldn't be rape.

"My poor girl – assaulted so near her home, and if you think this is going to be forgotten then you're very much mistaken," the woman declared.

Teddy began to get nervous. What was she getting at? What was her little game? Was she a cow or had he misjudged Fay?

"I think you had better come in, sit down and we'll have a chat don't you?" Teddy suggested.

Daisy took out a cigarette from her case which she assumed gave her more substance. Teddy felt that he should play for time.

"I haven't had my morning cup of coffee," he said. "As you are set on an argument, you'd better have one too."

Before she could respond, he disappeared into the kitchen and returned moments later with two cups of coffee.

"Now, what have we got to talk about?" Teddy smiled amicably at the woman.

"You screwed my daughter, got what you wanted and disowned her," Daisy declared flatly.

Teddy realised that this was a scheming and dangerous woman. She came from the wrong side of the tracks, and somehow he had to outwit her."

Daisy sipped her coffee and weighed up the room. Good, middle class she reasoned. He was younger than she had imagined and very good looking. His robe opened slightly to show a very muscular leg.

"Well, Mr. Teddy! You ravished my daughter, and what are you going to do about it?" Daisy demanded.

"What do you want me to do about it?" Teddy shrugged. "I walked your daughter home and we had a quick tumble on the way."

"A tumble was it?" Daisy glared at him. "That's an unusual name for it, I must say."

"Madam, your daughter was in it from the start – agreeable, willing from the start, and even begging for a quick fuck in the bushes," Teddy spelt it out for her. "She agreed, she happily asked for it and she enjoyed it as much as I did."

Daisy bristled. "My Fay was bruised and battered, and if that's your usual antics someone should hear about it. I read it in The Sun every day."

"I don't read papers like The Sun, Madam," said Teddy brusquely.

"Really, I think you have got your wires crossed. Boy meets girl, boy dates girl, they have a tumble, and she goes home. It's no fairy story but it will do."

"Oh, no it won't." Daisy was furious. "It won't do at all. Look Teddy, or whatever your name is. My girl is sixteen and a half and you know what the police and the newspapers will make of that!"

"She told me she was almost nineteen," protested Teddy.

"And I am the queen of the May," Daisy had to admit to herself she was quite enjoying this confrontation. "I'm afraid you behaved outrageously."

She gazed calculatingly up at the six foot male specimen and tapped her fingers on the arm of the chair. "I think a couple of grand will take care of it!"

This woman wanted two thousand pounds? As if he had it! Teddy thought quickly. In the top drawer of the cabinet was a bottle.

"That's blackmail!" he muttered.

"Call it what you like," Daisy stated, "but a couple of grand will keep me quiet for now!"

Teddy opened the bottle and took out a pill.

"Bloody hell, there's someone at the window." Teddy pointed at the window. "Look!"

Daisy turned but, of course, could see nothing. Meanwhile Teddy had dropped a tablet into her coffee.

"There's no one there!" she said.

"Are you sure?" asked Teddy.

"Positive. Now let's get down to business. She drank the remainder of her coffee. Two grand."

"I think you mean two thousand, Daisy."

Daisy suddenly became disturbed. Her head started spinning and so did the room at the same time.

Teddy knew the power of his tablet. It would render her dizzy, speechless and incoherent. Fay's mother suddenly lurched forward and was out for the count. Teddy was jubilant! Excited! Ecstatic!

Harry James had introduced him to this drug which was not unknown at the college, but this was the first time he had used it. Two grand indeed! The woman was insane and she wouldn't be able to remember a thing when she came round. Teddy started to undress Daisy, pulling off her trousers and interfering with her bra. At her age, she wasn't that bad looking and he wouldn't have minded giving her a 'tumble' as well as her daughter. He thought about it but decided against it. It would look better that he undid her clothing and took some photos to look as if she was doing the proposing. He got his camera and opened his robe. Carefully, he placed Daisy's bejewelled hand on his ample crotch and took a photo. Not bad, he thought. This was fun. He could do whatever he wanted. He became more and more inventive and soon had a dozen or more photographs taken in various positions. Teddy dressed himself and finished his now cold coffee. He waited for

27

the drug to wear off. Eventually Daisy groaned and sat upright.

"Christ! What the hell's going on?" Daisy tightened her bra, which was necessary as her ample bosom was spilling over the top. Her blouse was under the chair and her trousers were on the floor. Her mind was in a whirl, in a tangle. She tried in vain to recall where she was, who she was and why she was there? Why was she undressed? And who the hell was this man!

"That was fun," stated Teddy amicably.

"Why am I here?" Daisy stammered. "What am I doing here? Who are you?"

"Even strangers can be desirable to a lady like you," Teddy said suggestively.

"Oh! It's all coming back to me," gasped Daisy. "I want justice."

"You wanted me to fuck you!" Teddy declared. "You forced yourself on me and I have photos to prove it. You have been in the land of fantasy, trying to make me give you a considerable payment for a trumped up charge. Your daughter was not assaulted, raped or interfered with against her will. She was willing, able, and offered her body to be serviced like any other shop girl. Your demands for money are ludicrous. I think you should go home now. You do know where you live? Oh, and I think I have some great photos of our morning together," he smiled wickedly. "I particularly like the one of you with my dick in your mouth! If you come here again, you will find the photos all over the internet. I'll even send them to Fay. Let's see what she thinks of her sainted mother then!"

Daisy struggled into her clothes with difficulty.

"I think you had better go," Teddy said congenially. "I have things to do."

Daisy still didn't know exactly what she was doing, but Teddy helped her to the door.

"You won't have seen the last of me," she murmured.

"I can't wait," Teddy grinned. "I have such lovely photos to remember you by."

Teddy slammed the door after her. He had won this round, but would she be back, sometime, some day, somewhere?

***

Sam Silvester was nineteen and he wanted to lose his virginity. He wanted to proclaim to the world that he was worth a look, a man. He wanted to have it off with a girl, a woman, or a maiden. He was fairly tall, five foot nine, with a gentle face that was framed by a shock of auburn hair. Sam didn't have any courage or strength to help him achieve his ultimate goal. Teddy had put an advert in the local newsagent. The ad was a little hazy but intriguing and so Sam met up with Teddy at a nearby pub. Teddy outlined the adventure and he even had the audacity to use his sister on the receiving end. When Sam asked why his sister was such a willing young lady, Teddy covered it up by declaring that she was a very sexual woman and a woman of the world. What he failed to say was that she was a pretty young woman who would do anything to please her brother. She was a little dense in the brain department admittedly, but she was a good looking young girl. Sam worked as a clerk in a busy advertising office with a staff of ten. He found it difficult to join in and mix with them. They were all a bit older than Sam, and preferred their own company. They talked constantly about their affairs, their co-habiting, and their sexual antics. Sam was not sure whether they spoke the truth or not, especially Annabel, who apparently liked to be tied up like a prisoner. She was a girl who had seen too many movies and wanted a different kind of thrill.

Annabel, whose knockers were famous of their own accord, really thought she was the best fuck of all time.

Sam wanted experience. He was gentle, polite and altogether had much to recommend him. Sam had felt the need for sexual activity for some time. Masturbation was alright once in a while, but when it became a nightly necessity, it was a matter to be dealt with. He arranged an appointment with Teddy for four o'clock on the next Tuesday to meet Emma. He knew that he would be nervous, but then so might Emma.

Emma had created a new design, a butterfly, in all the beautiful colours of the rainbow. She was so pleased with her creation that she had completely forgotten the time. As the doorbell rang, she suddenly remembered the appointment that Teddy had arranged.

Emma dashed to the mirror, re-arranged her hair, put on a line of lipstick, and she was prepared. She wasn't expecting the very young and youthful Sam Silvester. Sam stood there nervously. Emma didn't quite know how to handle this but, as Teddy said, it would help pay the bills.

Emma liked Sam on sight. She could see he was nervous and did her best to put him at ease.

"Would you like some tea?" she asked.

"I would if that's alright," Sam replied nervously.

Emma smiled "Of course it is."

He looked at the beige carpet. "Do I have to take off my shoes?"

"No. It's far too early!" said Emma as she quickly went into the kitchen.

Suddenly, the doorbell rang again. Emma became flustered but went to the door just the same. It was Alice.

"Emma, I've baked a fruit cake and I thought you might like some with your tea. Oh! I'm sorry I didn't realise you had company."

Sam shifted nervously.

"This is Sam," said Emma.

"Pleased to meet you," said Alice.

"I did have an appointment you know," Sam stuttered.

"Well, that's alright," said Alice. She gave Emma the carefully foil-wrapped cake and said her goodbyes and left.

Sam didn't know what to say.

"Oh, we don't usually get anyone calling. Alice is an exception," said Emma, disappearing into the kitchen. "Go into the front room," she called out as she went.

Sam waited in the front room and suddenly spotted the colourful design on the side table. Emma entered with the tea.

"Goodness, that is lovely," Sam declared. "Did you do it?"

"It's a hobby of mine," Emma smiled sweetly. "I'm glad you like it."

Sam and Emma sat and looked at each other.

"You were expecting me?" Sam queried.

"Oh, yes. Teddy told me."

"Did he tell you that I was a virgin?" Sam asked.

"Yes," Emma replied nervously, "but what he didn't tell you was that I am too!"

Sam looked bewildered.

"I'm afraid I won't be very good," he began. "I felt that I had to get some experience or people will laugh at me."

"I won't laugh," Emma murmured.

"Thank you," Sam relaxed.

"Let's go upstairs," Emma suggested. "My bed is very comfortable."

"Good." Emma led Sam upstairs to her room at the back of the house.

"Shall I take my clothes off now?" said Sam coughing slightly.

"It might be a good idea."

Sam took off his coat, then, slowly, his trousers and shirt. Emma liked his briefs – all white and blue. She already had a liking for this young man.

She thought about what Teddy had said. He had told her to act naturally and one thing would lead to another.

Sam spoke. "Shall I keep my vest on?"

"If you like," Emma replied shyly.

Emma had dispensed with her dress. Her knickers wouldn't turn anyone on and her tits were small and round.

"Come on, Sam," she urged. "Let's go to bed."

Sam bristled and his penis started to rise. He did hope that Emma wouldn't be disappointed. He climbed in beside her.

"You can feel my breasts if you like," Emma whispered.

"Can I?"

"Of course." Emma was not sure what to do next. "The nipples are especially soft. Would you like to kiss them?"

"I know I've only got thirty minutes," Sam muttered anxiously.

"Is that what Teddy said?"

"Yes."

Emma took the nervous boy in her arms. This was nothing like she expected. She gave Sam a rapturous kiss, the closeness of her body sent shivers down his spine as he laid on top of her. Without realising it, he entered her and she let out a gasp of delight. Nature took over and they wallowed in a rapturous union. When it was done, they lay still for a few moments.

"Can we do it again?" asked Emma.

"I think we could, when I catch my breath," replied Sam. This was not what he had imagined. "Well, practice makes perfect they say."

Sam explored her young body, licking her pert breasts and slowly nibbling her hardening nipples. After a furtive fumbling, Sam suddenly burst out, "I've made a mess!"

"Did you enjoy it?" Emma asked.

"Actually yes, but what about you?"

"Teddy said it would just be normal," replied Emma, "but I think there's more to it than that."

"I'm sorry if you were disappointed," Sam muttered.

"Oh, no!" Emma exclaimed. "It's the first time for both of us. I think we will always remember this afternoon."

Sam got out of bed and started to dress. "Now, I'm a man!"

"Of course!" Emma smiled sweetly at him.

Sam looked at her tenderly. "You're far too nice to market yourself in this way, if I may say so, Emma."

"I won't do it often," promised Emma. "It was something like an experiment."

"I'm glad, Emma," Sam was sincere. "I'm so very glad. Do I give you the money?"

"Money?" Emma was puzzled. "I don't know anything about money."

"Teddy said it would be forty pounds."

"Oh!" He could see she couldn't add all this up.

"That's Teddy's department," Emma stated. "He deals with all the money."

"I'm really glad I met you," said Sam, "and I'm sorry about the sheets.

"Oh, don't worry. The washing machine is very useful."

Sam prepared to go.

"Can I see you again?" he asked. "I mean socially, so that we can have a talk – if your brother will let us."

"I don't know Sam, but I am so pleased to have met you," Emma replied.

"I've found a new friend."

"Do you have a telephone?"

"Yes."

"May I have the number?" Sam hoped to see this girl again.

Emma wrote the number on a piece of paper and gave it to him.

"There."

"What is the best time for me to ring?" he asked.

"The weekend would be best, I think. I don't seem to be very organised now that I haven't got my mother around."

Emma put on her dressing gown and followed him downstairs. Sam saw the drawing of the butterfly on the hall table where he had left it.

"I do like the butterfly," he said. "My office is promoting a new soap and they are looking for a logo."

"A soap?"

"Yes."

"Can I take this with me?" Sam asked.

"You can have it," Emma picked it up and pressed it into his hands. "I can always do another."

Sam kissed her gently on the cheek. "You won't forget me?"

"How could I forget you, Sam!"

"Goodbye, Emma."

With one last lingering look he went down the path and was gone.

***

Teddy was restless. He didn't know what was coming next. Alright, he seemed to have sorted Emma out, and made a few bob, and that could be ongoing. He looked through the local newspaper and found an advert which read 'Enterprising assistant required for a property firm'. It said to telephone Gloria Trent, and it gave a number. Teddy thought he would give it a go, nothing ventured, nothing gained. He rang the number and gave his name. An interview was arranged for eleven o'clock the following Friday. Several days later, Teddy had made another appointment for Emma. The man's name was Herbert Ramsey. Emma didn't want to think about it. She was slowly beginning to realise she was being used by Teddy. She couldn't get Sam out of her mind, but the payment issue troubled her.

***

Friday arrived and Teddy prepared for his interview with a certain Gloria Trent. He needed money, his hobbies were expensive, and he no longer had his mother to rely on.

He wore his grey suit with a sombre tie with gold specks all over it.

Looking in the mirror, Teddy was pleased with the result.

When he found the address, the office was first class. An elderly secretary ushered him in and there stood Gloria Trent. Teddy analysed the introduction. She was forty-five going on fifty. Her crisp blouse was home to enormous breasts, and her pencil thin skirt promised untold adventures.

It appeared that Gloria fronted a strong property firm that bought and sold flats and houses at an agreeable price. Gloria thought that a handsome young stud with an ample crotch could agreeably please property sellers, especially the wives of the clients. Gloria had married well. She and Wilfred Trent enjoyed a healthy living and a splendid bank account. Unfortunately, Wilfred had been crippled in a car crash, and now most of the running of the business was left to Gloria. The Gods had given her an attractive face, excellent eyes, and a personality to match. Her make-up was a little excessive and she wore her brown hair up, most days. She had married Wilfred some ten years ago. He was a good fifteen years her senior and before his accident, had been a wonder between the sheets.

Gloria found some of the running of the business a little wearisome.

A representative to show around prospective buyers was needed. She got bored with the routine, especially as most of the wives concerned were difficult to please, and argued constantly with their spouses.

She was as over sexed as she was tall. Life recently had been a drag.

She had never really loved Wilfred, but his money was a splendid compensation. Gloria found that Teddy was a most suitable applicant for the position. She instantly found him to be the very sort that she was looking for. Quite apart from his business acumen, his physical attributes were much to her liking. She could see much more than selling property might arise. It would, if she had anything to do with it!

***

Herbert Ramsey was middle-aged, a bachelor, and lived a solitary life with his parents. He was laid back, a trifle shy, and his parents and two sisters took little notice of him. They were too occupied with their own lives to bother with him.

His parents had always regarded him as an 'odd one'. He wore glasses and had little hair left on his bald head. He dressed soberly, was madly conservative, and his only interest was his work at the local library and his passion for literature. He didn't know why he had replied to Teddy's advertisement. Perhaps he had to live a little, or he had a need to find someone who would take an interest in him as a human being.

His needs were minimal especially in the bedroom department. His appointment with Emma was at three on a Sunday afternoon which was fine. He had made his appearance at church in the morning and had a meeting with his friend the vicar – another odd sheep in the pack.

Therefore, the afternoon was just right. Herbert lived his life in the books of Jane Austin, Daphne Du Maurier and such like.

Alice saw Herbert come to visit Emma. Again, her curiosity was paramount.

Emma, who never had been very social, seemed to be acquiring new friends or at least acquaintances! She was a very odd girl, strange in so many ways.

It was a cloudy day when Herbert arrived. There were dark clouds everywhere, and not a hint of clear sky or sunshine to be seen. He rang Emma's doorbell nervously not really knowing what to expect, secretly doubting his courage and reasons for coming. The door opened slowly and there stood Emma.

***

Teddy had been engaged by Gloria Trent and his first day arrived. He had taken great care once again; his wardrobe catered for his amazing body and his personality. The elderly assistant was nowhere to be seen, and Teddy could tell there were three rooms to the left of the office suite.

Gloria Trent went straight into the details of the job.

"I can take you on for a three month trial. We usually sell a property every two weeks or so. I can offer you five hundred pounds a week and, of course, a commission for each property you sell. My husband is rarely in the office, and prefers to work from home."

Teddy glowed. This was getting better by the minute. Gloria placed her hand on his biceps. "I must say you keep yourself in very good condition."

"I think I know my role in life, Mrs. Trent," Teddy tried to look modest.

"Gloria will do if we're going to work together," Gloria said. "Perhaps we should cement the arrangement over a drink."

Teddy smiled. "What a good idea!"

Gloria led the way into the adjoining office and closed the door.

It was brandy and a liberal portion. They both sat on the large Chesterfield settee which graced the room. Slowly, Gloria's hands ran over Teddy's body, especially his crotch. Then, suddenly, her lips were upon his, devouring as only a hungry passionate female could.

Her fervent hands quickly undid his belt and she desperately got rid of his trousers. She was amazed at what she found.

Soon, they were as naked as the Gods decreed. He lay on top of her, his erection was prominent, thick and long and worthy of a swordsman.

"I like it slow," she whispered. "I'm not into quickies."

"Then, slow it will be," said Teddy as he serviced her with delight.

She took his large manhood with ease and grunted her pleasure.

"Oh! That was good!" Gloria was delighted. "Now, we'll do it again. I like it both ways," and she turned over to lead the way. "I think we're going to get along rather well, Teddy, don't you?"

Teddy was stunned. This was a turn up for the books, but then in life, you never knew what was around the corner.

"I don't think that it's just property I'll be selling," he smiled at her wickedly.

***

Herbert sat down nervously in the large armchair in the front parlour.

"I really don't know why I am here," began Herbert "My name is Herbert Ramsey."

"I know," said Emma. "Do you want to undress a little while I make you a coffee?"

Herbert didn't know what came next but he knew with certainty that he couldn't possibly copulate with this woman. He wouldn't know what to do. He cased the room and it seemed quite familiar, and it pleased him somewhat. Emma brought in the coffee. "Two sugars?"

"Yes, please," he fumbled nervously.

"You haven't taken your trousers off," Emma commented. "We only have half an hour you know."

Herbert coughed nervously. "I haven't come for sexual gratification, Miss. I just wanted someone to talk to, and someone to talk to me. I live a very lonely life. I don't care about love and sex."

Emma didn't quite know how to handle this. She felt sorry for the lonely and unloved little man.

"Oh, that's all right Herbert," she said gently. "We can just talk if you prefer it. You can tell me what you do for a living, all about your family and what your interests are."

"Oh, Emma," he took her hand in his. "I'm not very interesting really, but I would like to talk to someone."

Emma suddenly realised that this little man had opened a door for her.

There are other things in life rather than sex, and she was grateful to know about life. Here was a lonely soul who no-one had time for, and she had time, lots of time.

Herbert sighed. "You really don't mind chatting to me?"

"Not at all," Emma took his hand in hers. "Now, what shall we talk about?"

"Well," Herbert began. "I'm very interested in books and authors. Will that do?"

"Of course," Emma replied, "and I can tell you all about me – except that there is not much to tell."

"I'll pay my money just the same," Herbert stated.

Herbert and Emma went into deep conversation, his eyes flickering with delight. Here was someone who had time for him. Little did he know that he was helping Emma as well as helping himself.

After Herbert had gone, (they had talked for more than an hour), Emma sat and thought. She thought that perhaps she was not so odd after all.

Suddenly, she was startled by the loud ringing of the telephone. It was Aunt Clara.

"Alice tells me you are having visitors, Emma!" Aunt Clara sounded annoyed. "I am coming down to find out what this is all about!"

***

Slowly, Emma was realising this was not what she was born to do.

Somehow, Teddy had misunderstood and demanded something from her that he shouldn't have. Aunt Clara would sort it all out.

Emma looked out on a gloomy landscape. She had a small breakfast, – small, because that was all she wanted. Teddy had eaten a huge breakfast and was preparing for his day.

"I've got a new job," he announced proudly.

"Oh!"

"Property," he declared.

"You mean houses and buildings?" Emma was impressed.

Teddy smiled. Emma was growing up. He hoped she would not ask too many questions.

"I show prospective clients around a flat, house, or mansion, and hopefully get them to buy it," Teddy explained.

"Oh!"

Teddy put on the jacket to his grey flannel suit. His crisp white shirt and carefully patterned tie really did look good.

"See to the laundry, will you Emma, there's a good girl," he ordered.

"In your new job, will you be earning money for us – I mean to pay the bills?" Emma asked.

Teddy smiled. "Oh, my money will help enormously, and you are doing your share. I think Frazer is coming to see you today."

"Yes, Teddy," Emma murmured. "But, will I have to work much longer? You said it was just an experiment."

"Did I?" Teddy avoided her eyes. "We'll talk about it tonight."

With that he was gone.

Alice was in the front room when she saw Teddy leave. She wasn't always nosey, but she had to admit that the gentlemen she saw visiting Emma were an odd bunch. The whole thing was a puzzle. Was Teddy trying to set up a club, or establish some kind of business?

Alice sighed. It was now some time since poor Rose had passed away and the goings on next door would have to wait. She had things to do, shopping, and plans for the weekend. She thought she might call in on Emma a little later on.

***

Teddy arrived at the property early. It was a fairly ordinary house, at least, it was detached, and not in a terrace. A Mr. and Mrs. Baker were coming to look it over. They met Teddy on the stroke of twelve, not a minute early, not a minute late. Mrs Baker was a nondescript woman of forty-five going on fifty. Mr. Baker was the usual provincial husband who would agree to anything for a quiet life.

Teddy did his job well. He was the perfect salesman and Martha Baker noted that he had much to offer. He showed them around and then he showed them around again in greater detail.

"Not bad," said Martha. "But then, we have more houses to see."

"I think it is what we are looking for," said George Baker. "I don't see why we should want to see more properties, although a larger garden would be nice I suppose."

"Why don't you have another look around, George, whilst I talk to this young man."

"All right, Martha," he muttered as he trundled dutifully off to measure the garden.

"I do like it," she declared "The kitchen could be larger, and the guest bedroom needs decorating; I personally can't bear pale green when I wake up in the morning."

"Quite." Teddy could see Martha was not in the mood to like anything, except perhaps himself!"

"You look as if you do some modelling, Teddy. You wear clothes so well."

"Thank you, that's kind. I do go to the gym quite a lot," Teddy admitted.

George returned rather quickly, which did not suit Martha at all.

"We'll take it!" he said to Teddy.

"We won't!" said Martha. "There are other houses to see and explore."

She put her hand on Teddy's and looked at him through grey eyes trying to look young. "I take it, Teddy, that you will always be around to show us more properties."

"Oh, I expect so!" said Teddy cautiously.

"I think I will insist." She winked as she put a piece of paper in Teddy's hand.

"I'll ring Gloria Trent to say I'm not sure about this one."

George grunted. "I knew you'd fuss, Martha."

"I don't fuss, but I've got to live in the house for evermore, and it has got to be right. You do see my point, young man?"

"Certainly, decisions like this always take time." Teddy smiled knowingly.

"They always do with her," said George, pointing to his unattractive wife.

"Well, we'd better go," said Martha as she left. "I will look forward to hearing from Gloria Trent about other houses which are for sale."

She gave Teddy a rapturous smile and dragged George down the garden path.

Teddy shook his head. That was a waste of time, he thought, but what was the note she had pressed into his hand? He opened it gingerly.

It read: **Why don't you pop round to my house one morning? I'm sure we have much more in common. Much love, Martha!**

"Oh! Christ!" muttered Teddy. Perhaps his Emma wasn't the only one providing a service.

Wilfred Trent cursed every breaking day. He could no longer control his business and he could not satisfy his rampant wife, Gloria. When he had married her, their bedroom had been an arena for sexual play.

She had demanded and he had supplied. She had come into his life and had quickly learnt his trade. Her tenacity was remarkable, her salesmanship superb and it got better all the time. She definitely knew how many beans made five! From the start she had made Wilfred's sex life superb. She knew angles and positions that would please an experienced woman of the street. Although Wilfred had never been a looker, the two seemed to gel perfectly. She had managed to introduce Wilfred to a new avenue in the world of intercourse. At that time he was fairly tall, with a nondescript face and eyebrows that tended to be bushy. One could say he was rather plain, already with a little tummy and his face regularly sported pimples and a sudden rash. However, his apparatus would please every sexual maiden in the telephone book.

Long ago, a woman called Mae West had decreed that sex was here to stay, and that woman had never said a truer word.

Wilfred's driver, Richard, had been with him for years; a sturdy youth, tall in the saddle, who felt that his equipment was to be admired. Wilfred liked him a lot, and Richard basked in this knowledge. Wilfred could have been bi-sexual but now, since the accident, the universe would never know.

The accident had happened on a day when birds sang and the world woke early at seven o'clock and ambitious people plotted their day. He had been to inspect some houses, in fact an entire terrace, on the right side of Fulham. Each house had three bedrooms and was in tip top condition. The day had been immensely rewarding, and Wilfred was pleased. He was so delighted that he ordered Richard to stop at the next public house, The Cat and Fiddle. Richard looked the part with his linen suit and coloured tie. He could be mistaken for an associate of Wilfred's or even his son. They both enjoyed their quiet drink at The Cat and Fiddle and emerged a little merrier than before. A black four wheel drive motor appeared from nowhere from a side road and crashed into Wilfred's limousine. The car crumpled and the two men were injured. The owner of the other car was killed instantly. The ambulance came and Wilfred and Richard were taken to a nearby hospital. Richard had minor injuries, which healed in double quick time, no doubt helped by his fitness and youth.

However, Wilfred had had to remain in hospital for a good few weeks.

His spine was broken, his ribs crushed and, all in all, the doctors who attended him were to be congratulated on keeping him alive.

So, Wilfred's life had changed dramatically. Luckily, due to Gloria's aptitude for business, the firm carried on regardless. Wilfred had to take the role of a bystander, but of course, he could chronicle the day to day life of Gloria Trent. Richard stayed in their employ and Gloria, looking at this good looking young man, could only imagine the delights that he might offer. She would keep him in reserve for a rainy day.

***

Unknown to Teddy, in fact unknown to the whole world, was the fact that Emma kept a diary. Emma thought that everyone kept a diary, and so she chronicled her thoughts and deeds daily. The one thing that she was proficient at was drawing. She could illustrate her day, and painted her world in watercolour and oils. She drew the insects in the garden, the tortoise that lived underneath the tree in the garden, and the four pigeons that she fed every morning with breadcrumbs. Her drawings were quite unique and she took much pleasure from them. She realized that this may seem mundane to others but it was her diary.

It was the details of her life, her day, and it belonged to her and no one else. She recorded the visits of the different men who had called upon her. Each one was different, a new variety, and she described them all perfectly, in great detail. She knew Teddy wasn't interested in diaries or books. In fact, she didn't know what interested him at all, but many women could have told her exactly what did!

Emma hoped the experiment would end soon. She had learnt something about her body, about men, about urges and human requirements.

She didn't really understand about births of any kind, or how the world evolved. She was content with her own little world. Her knowledge was sparse, she didn't know much, and what she didn't know, she imagined.

Emma's appetite wasn't remarkable. She was a slim, timid, young woman, and her long, dark hair framed a very pretty face. She was a puzzle, a mystery. She mused that Teddy's little game had to be short-lived. Experiments always were.

***

Emma had experienced two quiet days. She had been glad of the leisure with no demands on her, and enjoyed being left to do what she liked. Her art was progressing. Her design the day before had been a cloud that suddenly developed into a shawl of many colours, a rapturous blend of blues, greys, and a dark shade of crimson.

Teddy had told her that, on this particular morning, a famous man would call for attention. It was a Tuesday. Emma liked Tuesdays. She didn't know why but she did. The man had apparently featured in forgotten movies and was into writing. Perhaps he wrote about his experiences.

He was quite a heart-throb and certainly not a man to be ignored. Emma didn't know. She hadn't been to the cinema since her mother had taken her to see Snow White.

Teddy had liked Frazer on sight. He was handsome, just thirty years old, but had done the rounds and then some. Frazer was going places.

Everyone said so. Teddy said so, and so did Frazer! Teddy could smell gold wherever Frazer went.

Emma was getting tired of this 'experiment'. The past few months since her mother died had flashed by. Moreover, Emma's devotion to Teddy was beginning to fade.

The doorbell rang. It was Frazer Lloyd. He was blonde, tall, about six foot four, and had twinkling eyes in his warm handsome face. His smile would have excited a nun and his personality stunned Emma. He had a sturdy yet slim body, and Emma knew the moment that he came in that he was different.

"No wonder he's famous," thought Emma. Why had he bothered to visit her? Surely he could release his sexual favours to grateful ladies the country over.

"Hello," said Emma.

"Hi! I'm Frazer!"

"I'm Emma. I am expecting you."

He smiled and she ushered him quickly into the front room. He sat in the armchair and spread his long legs widely as he quickly surveyed the room.

"Would you like some tea?" she enquired.

"I think tea with a little fornication would be satisfactory," he winked mischievously.

"I won't be a moment," Emma rushed to the kitchen.

Frazer had been introduced to Teddy by Gloria Trent. Gloria had met Frazer and seduced him whilst working as an extra on a film many moons ago. Frazer soon saw through Teddy's game, and decided when he saw the advertisement, that he would look into this situation.

He felt Teddy was playing a dangerous game, and somewhere he thought there was a film or a book in this story. In spite of his good looks, he was not that magical in the sex game, and he knew it.

Emma brought in the tea.

"Sugar?" she asked.

"Certainly not, I have my figure to think about. Teddy told you I was coming?"

"You're in the diary."

Frazer took his tea and stirred the cup although there was no reason to do so as he didn't take sugar.

"Do you like being famous?" Emma was digging although she didn't know why. Emma and Frazer sat there, the matinee idol and the obliging female, a combination not exactly made in heaven.

"Shall we go to the bedroom?" he asked.

"Follow me," said Emma with a smile.

They went upstairs to her room.

Frazer gave her a wide smile as he took off his cowboy boots, and slowly his trousers. He sat on the bed in just his shirt.

"Shall we begin?" he asked.

"Why not!" she liked Frazer and his famous good looks was the icing on the cake. She slowly took off her dress and the splendour of her body was pleasing. Her small youthful breasts were absolutely right for her slight and rounded frame. He slipped off his shirt and the excellence of his body astounded her. Tiny blonde hairs decorated his glistening chest. Emma could not explain the feeling she was experiencing. She was enjoying this!

They both got on the bed and he started to caress her nipples. His tongue gave her a tingling feeling as he gradually worked his way down her body.

His manhood was definitely pleased to see her. His body odour was something again – so different, so clean, natural and so exciting.

Emma glowed and clasped his head tenderly in her hands.

Suddenly Frazer sat up!

"I'm afraid I'll have to go now," he declared. "Sorry about that. You are a lovely, sweet girl and we must meet again. I'd like to take you out to dinner one evening."

"Oh!" Emma was so surprised. "But you haven't had what you came for!"

"I have," Frazer replied. "I wanted to meet you and know how I rate in your list of clients."

Emma blushed. "We haven't…"

"No, we haven't," Frazer smiled, "but we've met and I think you are lovely. How do I rate, Miss Jones?"

"Oh! I couldn't tell you that! It's a secret!" Emma cried. "I'm sorry you haven't had your money's worth. I don't know what Teddy will say."

"Teddy won't say anything," Frazer said firmly. "This is certainly between you and me, Emma. You must learn that the label doesn't always match the parcel."

Frazer secretly loathed Teddy, and his unscrupulous hobby of exploiting his sister. He was enraged within and promised to teach Teddy a lesson he wouldn't forget. Frazer dressed quickly and Emma put her dress back on.

"Emma, I have to go," Frazer said apologetically. "You don't know how great it has been meeting you. I'll ring you, if I may, and that dinner we shall have."

"I'll have to ask Teddy," Emma demurred.

"No, he'll ask for more money," Frazer declared firmly. "No, my sweet Emma, this is a secret between you and I." He kissed her tenderly and was gone. After Frazer had gone, Emma sat thinking. Why did she feel this way?

What the hell was the matter with her? She didn't recognise feelings like this, and why did Frazer register so well? There was so much she didn't know. Her life was suddenly spinning, as she became more aware of who she was, what she was doing, and what she must try to change. Her mother was not here to advise and guide her. She was so alone, so isolated. Teddy lived in a different world, another place.

Then she remembered Sam, young Sam. She had liked Sam, and he liked her drawings and had even taken one. Perhaps Teddy wouldn't book in any more callers, and she would be able to wear what she liked.

Somehow, today, she was happy and she drifted off on a cloud of dreams. Nothing really made sense, not today, not tomorrow, perhaps never. Frazer got into his car and thought, 'my God, this is going to make a bloody good book perhaps even a film, and I'm going to make Emma rich!'

***

Alice was worried if not a little anxious. This last month, Emma had received, to her knowledge, several visitors – all men. They had all stayed about half an hour. Perhaps it was none of her business but she thought Emma may need more help to see her through the day.

She had always been fragile, and she would be missing her mother.

So, Alice helped her with her shopping, bought the produce at the right price, at the right shops, and she thought that Emma was improving a little. Emma's health had always been a worry for poor Rose, and the paucity of intelligence was also always a worry. Sometimes she seemed to be improving, to accept life as it should be, and then another day she would slip back again to the backward young woman Alice had known.

Teddy was no help. He went his own way and she gathered his prowess with the local girls would fill a book. Whether or not he could be trusted, she couldn't tell. He was well-educated, nobody's fool and with his outstanding looks and build, he was very popular.

She knew Emma adored her brother, but whether that was reciprocated was another matter.

Alice was a nice, normal, provincial soul. She asked for nothing, and she had no ambition save keeping house and looking after her husband.

Joe. They had been together for forty years. He worked as a bookie for a large firm, and had a regular wage which was more than enough to keep them in comfort. Alice had married Joe when she was seventeen. She had fallen for this young man like a ton of bricks, and she had never regretted it for an instant. He was kind, thoughtful, took her abroad once a year for a holiday, and their only regret was that she had been unable to conceive and produce a child. Her nephew, Robert came and stayed with her regularly. He was a sharp, knowing lad, and very little escaped him. He had been down to stay with her recently for a few days, and he had alerted Alice that something was amiss next door.

Alice had thought much the same. Alice and Rose had been very close.

Alice was much more than a neighbour and she had helped Rose to conquer the many problems that had beset her through the years, with the task of bringing up Emma.

Robert had mentioned his concerns to Alice during his recent stay.

"Emma seems to have acquired some male friends, Aunt Alice," he had said.

"Yes, I was thinking the same thing," Alice had agreed. "If this is the case, I am glad for her as there is not much in life for the poor girl stuck in that house all day."

Robert sighed. "It's none of my business, but the age groups don't make sense. I think I know the last chap, I've seen him on television or somewhere, of that I am sure."

After Robert went home, Alice thought long and hard. Robert was right and he had agreed with her that things were not as they should be. So, Alice had decided to telephone Aunt Clara. She was a woman that she did not take to very easily, and she inwardly thought that Clara could have done more to help her sister Rose.

She knew that she had Clara's number somewhere and she tipped out her drawer and there it was. "Clara Sullivan," and the number. Alice's husband had reservations on the matter.

"Dear, it's not really your business," he admonished. "Emma is almost grown up and must build her own life. Besides which, Teddy is there to make sure that everything is all right."

Alice scowled. "That could be a disadvantage if you ask me."

"Well Alice, you must do what your heart dictates. My advice to you is to let things go their own way." Joe put on his hat and coat and went off to the office. Alice downed her second cup of tea and made up her mind. Clara must be told.

***

Clara was not a woman to lie in bed, and was up with the dawn. Her husband did as he was told, which, in fact, he was happy to do and the two went their separate ways. Clara belonged to three different clubs in the village, and was always organising everyone, and overruling most people's opinions. She gave manipulation a bad name.

Alice telephoned Clara's number and she answered immediately. It was as if she had been waiting for the call all day.

"Yes, seven five seven four. Oh, it's you Alice," Clara greeted her.

"At this time of day, it must be something urgent."

Alice expressed her concern as well as she could.

"Well!" said Clara. "Not much can be wrong with that layabout Teddy there, but I must admit it does seem strange. Perhaps Emma has grown up at last and managed to mingle and meet a few people. Well, in any case, I was planning to come down. I always worry about Emma and what the future holds for her. Thank you for phoning, Alice."

Aunt Clara put down the phone and the conversation ended.

Alice was pleased that she had made the effort, and now she could rest assured that nothing was going to go wrong for Emma.

***

Emma was up early on the Monday. She had breakfast with Teddy who didn't give her any appointments, and so Emma had the day free to continue with her art. She had assembled more designs into a book, and she was extremely proud of her efforts. At eleven o'clock on the dot, Aunt Clara arrived. With her pillbox hat sitting securely on her head, she looked very much like the wicked Queen from Snow White.

"Now, how has life been, Emma?" Aunt Clara asked. "I presume Teddy has been looking after you."

Emma gave her a worried look and started to tremble.

"What is it, Emma?" Aunt Clara softened. "I'm here to help."

"I don't know where to begin, Aunt Clara."

Clara waited. "The start is always a step in the right direction," she stated firmly.

"I will make the tea and then I think you will have something to tell me."

Emma smiled nervously.

***

They drank the tea that Clara had made. "You take sugar, don't you, Emma."

"Yes, Aunt," Emma coughed nervously.

"Now, Emma," Aunt Clara said firmly. "I think you could have something to tell me, my girl. I hear that you have had several visitors."

"Yes, Aunt Clara."

"Why have visitors all of a sudden?" Aunt Clara demanded.

Emma started to cry and gradually Clara got to the bottom of the sad affair.

"Teddy said it was an experiment," Emma sobbed.

"I'm sure he did!" Aunt Clara looked shocked. "An experiment that ceases immediately!" She took Emma's hand in hers. "Thank goodness your mother is not around to hear this mess."

Gradually Aunt Clara got all the facts out of Emma, who dried her tears and attempted to control herself. The front door slammed and Teddy came in.

"Why Aunt Clara, what a surprise!" he declared brightly. "I didn't know you were coming."

"I'm sure you didn't," said Aunt Clara standing tall, and dominating the room.

"Sit down!" she commanded. "I've got some words to say to you."

Aunt Clara ranted and raved and Teddy tried to cover up his sins.

"I was trying to bring Emma up-to-date," he offered, "to acknowledge the world as it were."

Aunt Clara coloured. "How dare you lie!" she glared at him. "You were making money, using your sister for sex with strangers. People have been hung for less."

Emma made to leave the room.

"Emma," Aunt Clara's voice softened, "go out into the garden while I deal with this ghastly affair."

Emma gave her a wan smile and obeyed.

"Now, Teddy Jones," Aunt Clara glared at him. "I want you out of this house by the weekend. Is that clear?"

Teddy didn't like her tone. "You are in no position to throw me out!" he shouted.

"Let me remind you. This is my house, and Emma's, and what do you know about sex anyway?"

"I have been married for many years," Aunt Clara snapped.

"Yes, your old man must have been desperate," Teddy muttered angrily.

"You had better gather your things together and be gone by Saturday morning, and that's my final word!" Aunt Clara ordered.

Teddy scowled. "We'll see about that."

"Yes we will," Aunt Clara declared with venom. "Perhaps you'd prefer a prison cell instead, would you? That wouldn't be a problem!"

Teddy got up and scowled. "As if you'd know! I've got things to do."

"You've never said a truer word," Aunt Clara dismissed him.

Teddy stormed out.

Aunt Clara called Emma in from the garden.

"Now, Emma," she said gently, "you won't have any more gentlemen callers, that I can promise you."

"Yes, Auntie."

There was a knock at the back door. Clara called "Come in!"

It was Alice, dying to know the outcome of the morning.

"Well?" began Alice.

"You were right. We do have a problem, but I will sort it out. I will come down here for a while to look after Emma, and that's that!"

"Oh!" Alice paused. "What about Teddy?"

"He can get somewhere else to live, or he'll know the consequences. I will not beat about the bush. We have this poor girl to think about. I'm a woman who speaks her mind."

Alice thought that no one would argue with that!

"When I captain a ship, I can assure you that everything will turn out well. You can take my word for it," Aunt Clara declared firmly. "Discussion closed!"

Chapter Two

Teddy sat down to think. He had been thrown out of his house. He was angry. After all, half of it was his. He would have to think about this.

Meanwhile, he must get on well with Gloria Trent in one way or another. Teddy had been trying to fix the sale of a bungalow that belonged to two sisters. Teddy reported back to Gloria who was impressed to see Teddy so efficient. The ladies hadn't argued, and were just delighted. Gloria could definitely see that they would have a sale for the bungalow.

Gloria had experienced a rather lousy day and she liked to report to her husband Wilfred when she had enjoyed a good one. However, she still had the hots for Teddy.

"You feel we have a sale?" she asked.

"Yes, definitely," Teddy replied. "I don't know if they were actually sisters or just lovers."

"I don't care what religion they are!" said Gloria with a smile.

She kissed Teddy on the cheek and put one hand on his body, where she shouldn't have!

Teddy grinned naughtily. "Anything happening?"

"Nothing planned," Gloria replied suggestively, "but then, perhaps you have to hurry things along a bit."

Her hand lingered wickedly on his crotch. "Time for a quickie?"

Teddy glowed. "Why not!" He was pleased he was scoring so well with Gloria, and it was giving his vanity a lift. She could be useful in more ways than one. She led him into the inner office where she had introduced him originally and quickly undid his jeans. A moment later, they were both naked and the sofa had guests again. Gloria was delighted. Teddy was a good salesman, his extra service was constant and his size and prowess to be admired.

As Teddy put on his shirt, he casually posed his question.

"We have several flats empty at the moment, and one nearby."

"Yes, why do you ask?"

"Well, I need a pad for a few weeks as the builders want to renovate mine," Teddy explained.

"Well," Gloria thought for a moment. "I suppose I could let you have the flat next door. Only temporary you understand."

"Could we say for services rendered?" he ventured.

"We could," Gloria smiled. "It might be handy, if you know what I mean."

"I know what you mean, Gloria," Teddy was delighted. "I'm a man who never misses a trick. I promise you, you won't be sorry."

"No, I don't think I will, but discretion is a necessary thing," Gloria warned.

"I am a married lady you know."

"And a very experienced one I may add." Teddy went to pull on his trousers when a note fluttered to the floor.

"What's that?" said Gloria as she picked it up.

"Just a telephone number," Teddy said quickly.

"I know, but it does seem familiar!" Gloria murmured.

Teddy grabbed the note from her hand. "Too much knowledge can be a dangerous thing."

"Too true," said Gloria as the telephone rang and she went to answer it.

***

The afternoon had no commitments, so Teddy decided to telephone the number on the piece of paper. Martha answered "Oh! It's you Teddy. What a surprise."

"I just wondered if you were free this afternoon?"

"As a matter of fact I am!" said Martha, breathless with excitement.

"Why don't you come round?"

Teddy smiled. Business was really busy! "In an hour?" he suggested.

"In an hour," Martha agreed.

Teddy looked at his watch. He needed a shower, but that would have to wait. He drove round to Martha's. She was as good as her word. She greeted him as if she had known him all her life.

"This is a nice surprise, I must say," she began.

"I'm really glad you think so," Teddy replied. "I am so pleased that you are taking the new house. You couldn't have made a better decision."

"I hope you're right."

"Do you mind if I use your bathroom?" Teddy asked. "If I could have a shower that would be great; the house I was seeing over this morning really needed a spring clean."

"It's a bit unusual! But I don't see why not."

Martha led him to the bathroom. "Help yourself, clean towel on the left."

"Thank you," said Teddy winking at her.

Teddy ran the shower and soon the hot water was cruising all over his muscular body. He thought Martha was not the best thing ever, but although she was plain, she could be very grateful. He took his time and when he was drying himself before the mirror, the door slowly opened. There she was, Martha, as naked as the day she was born!

"I thought you might need a little help." she said as she led him into the bedroom. She lay on the bed with her legs apart waiting for Teddy to climb aboard. Martha might have been plain, but her vigour and energy was amazing. It all turned out so much better than he imagined.

She knew exactly how to worship his body, not once but twice. How could he not oblige?

Suddenly, the door opened and there stood her husband.

"So you're at it again!" said George as he ran his eyes over Martha's body. Then he turned on Teddy, who quickly lost his erection.

"Alright, Tarzan!" muttered George angrily as he leapt at the naked Teddy.

George dragged Teddy off the bed, grabbing his body at an unfortunate angle. He almost swung Teddy around the room.

"I'll give you something to remind you of Martha," George said, as he landed a vicious blow on Teddy's right eye. Teddy was very shaken up.

"Now, go and sell your wares somewhere else." George gave Teddy a swift and very precise kick up the backside.

"Get some clothes on and get out!" George was quite enjoying this as Teddy scrambled out of the door, grabbed his clothes from the bathroom, and left as quickly as he could.

George turned to Martha. "It seems we won't be moving after all, sweetie. Now let us see what we can do to a naughty girl like you." The bedroom door closed slowly and firmly.

Teddy had a black eye for a week and he lost the sale of the house.

***

By the Saturday, as decreed by Clara, Teddy had packed his three suitcases and his wardrobe was fairly empty. Emma was sad to see him go, but on the other hand, she was relieved; she would not have to copulate with any more men. She did however have Clara to deal with. It was not going to be easy, but life never was, at least not for Emma.

Alice came round as usual to take Emma shopping.

"Things have taken a sudden turn, Emma," Alice said. "I never thought in a million years that Teddy would move out, and Clara would move in."

Emma looked puzzled. "Teddy said it was only temporary! He has only taken some of his clothes."

Alice and Emma did their shopping and enjoyed their coffee and biscuits which was their normal routine after shopping. Back home, the telephone rang and Emma got up to answer it. It was Sam.

"Would it be alright if I can come round?" he asked nervously.

"What time?" Emma smiled. She liked Sam.

"What about now?" he asked. "I'm only around the corner."

"All right, Sam, it will be nice to see you."

Alice was all ears. "What's his name?"

"Oh, Sam Stevenson," Emma replied. "You met him once when he came round."

"I think I had better go," said Alice.

"No, please stay."

"Then I will," Alice decided, "but I don't want to be in the way."

Emma was puzzled. What did Sam want? There was no one booked in, so it couldn't be that! Anyway, with Clara moving in there wouldn't be any of that again!

Alice was curious. "Have you continued with your art design?"

"Oh, yes." Emma was pleased with her interest. "I did six more designs last week. Can I show them to you?"

"Please do." Alice loved Emma's work.

Emma went to the cupboard and brought out the large scrapbook.

She opened it and Alice saw the tremendous multitude of colours.

"Emma, these are wonderful!" Alice was amazed. "Are you sure you did them all by yourself?"

"Oh, yes."

A moment later, the doorbell rang. "I'll go," said Alice.

A moment later, Alice ushered in young Sam. He seemed very nervous, but was obviously delighted to see Emma again. Emma introduced him again to Alice.

"You've been here before," Alice remarked.

"Yes, just the once."

"And what are you here for?" Alice asked pointedly.

Sam hesitated. He didn't know how to play this, but Emma chipped in to save his embarrassment.

"I'm glad you remembered the address," Emma smiled.

"Alice – he had an appointment, and he liked my butterfly designs," Emma explained. "He even took one away with him."

"She's done some more," added Alice, pointing to the scrapbook.

Sam excitedly poured over Emma's work.

"The colours are splendid, Emma," he commented, "and they are all different butterflies."

"I like butterflies," explained Emma. "They are so colourful and delicate and never do anyone any harm."

"Quite." Alice thought she should find out some more about this man.

"But what's your interest Sam?"

"I work for an advertising & promotional company," Sam replied.

"They provide material to highlight various goods."

"Have you been there long?" asked Alice.

"A year and three days," Sam replied.

"You're very precise," Alice laughed.

"I'm sorry," Sam shrugged, "but that's the way I am."

"There's nothing to be sorry about, Sam." Alice relaxed. "I am glad that Emma has got a friend."

"I only saw one design when I was here before," said Sam, "but you have worked on so many others since I saw you last. What does your brother say?"

There was an ominous silence. "Oh, he doesn't live here anymore," Alice declared at last.

Both Alice and Sam looked ill at ease.

"What is your interest in butterflies, Sam?" Alice asked.

Sam coughed nervously.

"I know it is a bit pretentious of me," Sam coughed nervously, "but I was telling my boss, Mr. Butler, about the wonderful colours and designs Emma had done with her butterfly painting. He asked me if I could show him more. Would you agree to do that, Emma?"

Emma didn't know how to handle this, but Alice stepped in with gusto.

"Of course she would, Sam. It's very nice of you to take such an interest."

"Design is what my company does."

"Do you want to take the whole book?" asked Alice.

"Could I, Emma?" Sam's eyes gleamed with excitement.

Emma didn't look pleased.

"You might lose the book, or get it lost or stolen," she declared uneasily.

"What would I do then?"

"Oh, I'd take good care of it I promise, Emma," Sam pleaded. "I will guard it with my life."

"Then you shall have it, Sam," Alice intervened, "but I would like the name of your company, the telephone number and your name and address."

"Of course, I have my card somewhere." Sam rummaged in his pocket and produced his business card.

Emma looked puzzled. She was sad to see her scrapbook taken away.

"I'll bring it back," Sam promised, giving Emma a funny look. "I won't have to have an appointment, will I?"

"No," said Emma. "Teddy isn't doing appointments anymore."

Alice looked uncomfortable.

"I am so glad," said Sam.

"So am I," said Emma and she really meant it.

"I'd better go now," said Sam as he gathered up the scrapbook and put it in his rucksack.

"How long will you keep Emma's book?" asked Alice.

"I really don't know, Alice," Sam replied. "Sometimes they get round to things quite quickly, and other times, they take weeks or even months."

"I will be lost without it," Emma remarked sadly.

"Then I'll get you another book and you can do some more." Alice put her arm around Emma's shoulder. "Of course you will miss your scrapbook, but the chance to show off your work is encouraging. You must continue with your drawings, Emma. I will tell your Aunt Clara about them."

Emma became more upset.

"Oh, no! Not Aunt Clara! She'll not understand. She could forbid me to draw!"

Sam looked bewildered. What on earth was this all about?

"Clara will do no such thing," Alice declared reassuringly. "Underneath her harsh exterior is a kindly soul. She wouldn't dream of stopping you. As you get to know her more, you will find much to admire."

Emma still looked as if she was going to cry.

"Emma's Aunt Clara is coming to look after her," Alice explained to Sam.

Sam took Emma's hand gently.

"Don't cry, Emma. Everything will be ok. I'll let you have the book back quite soon."

"Of course he will," said Alice.

"Anyway, I have got to go now, ladies," Sam said. "I really have things to do."

"It was nice to meet you again Sam," said Alice.

"Thank you Ma'am," said Sam.

"See you soon."

Sam left with his rucksack, and Emma's scrapbook. Soon afterwards, Alice also had to leave, leaving Emma alone with her thoughts.

***

Gloria was not impressed with the black eye that Teddy featured after his incident with Martha. Teddy looked rather sheepish, and Gloria pursed her lips. Perhaps he had met his match.

"It's almost going home time," she murmured as she carefully surveyed his crotch.

Teddy bent down to pick up a piece of paper that had missed the litter bin and she admired his tight, attractive arse.

"Shall we have a drink, Teddy?" she asked.

Teddy knew where the drink would lead and, in no time at all, they were in the next room and were at it like rabbits. Gloria was almost screaming with pleasure as he lay on top of her and Teddy satisfied her once again, both sides – even with a black eye!

Back at home, Wilfred had been going through his books and properties.

"It could be better," he told Richard.

"I thought I could count on offloading that house yesterday. They seemed the right couple, and they were interested."

Richard poured Wilfred a whisky.

"Gloria had the new boy, Teddy, handling the job," Wilfred said. "Perhaps he isn't the strong representative we imagined. What do you make of him Richard?"

"Well," said Richard "I've only seen him once. He's about six foot tall, about twenty-one, and quite handsome in a roguish way."

"Oh!" Wilfred was deep in thought. "I know Gloria offered him a good commission on the place, so I did expect a sale. Would you find him attractive?"

Wilfred liked to know where everyone was and why.

"As I said," Richard replied guardedly, "he's very good looking."

"I must say, I've never seen Gloria so enthusiastic for many a day," Wilfred muttered crossly. "Oh, I hate to be in this bloody state, Richard, if only I had my legs. The fact I can't satisfy Gloria in the bedroom department is another thing. You have no idea how frustrating all this is for me."

Richard was immediately attentive. He took Wilfred's hand and played with his fingers.

"I know you understand, Richard," Wilfred sighed.

"Oh, I do," whether Richard liked Wilfred or his millions was a mystery, but he was very attentive.

"I think I want you to do a little investigation," Wilfred declared suddenly.

"Gloria has a great capacity for sex. When we first got together, intercourse three times a day was the norm. She could get me excited so quickly, so totally. She was a tornado...and look at me now."

Richard sat beside him and gave him a warm kiss, as though it was expected.

"Yes, a little investigation is what we need," Wilfred repeated. "What do you say Richard?"

"I will look into it tomorrow," Richard promised.

Richard was good to Wilfred, and Wilfred noticed his build, tight rear and his appendage. He has a lot going for him, thought Wilfred. It took all kinds to make a world, and who was Wilfred to disagree.

Richard answered the advertisement that Wilfred had put in 'The Gazette' several years back. 'Young man wanted, must drive, PA to local business man.'

Richard came from a poor family, and had three sisters. His mother still worked and his father was a non-event. He had such a basic education that it did not help him when seeking employment. But, he had a great personality and the one good thing that his father had done was teach him how to drive.

This was just what the doctor ordered when he was interviewed by Wilfred. His interview was on a Tuesday. Richard had chosen his wardrobe carefully. He had worn a smart checked suit, white shirt and a blazing red tie. His shoes had been of a black and white variety, very similar to the ones Fred Astaire favoured in the thirties. His trousers had been extremely tight, both back and front and his body was to be admired when he took off his jacket. He was twenty-five and he had been around. In his teens, he had discovered sex and his equipment had been enjoyed by both boys and girls. His main problem was commitment. He just didn't want to be contracted, organised or hitched to another for better or for worse.

So, when Wilfred's interview came up it seemed to be just right for him. Of course he was not the only applicant. In fact, Wilfred saw five other applicants for the job. He was looking for something special and Richard seemed to fit the bill.

Richard and Wilfred got on immediately. Although Wilfred couldn't figure so strongly in his property business after the car crash, it didn't do any harm to continue to have a driver and assistant with good looks.

Wilfred had luck early in life. He had started with fifty thousand pounds that his father had left him in the middle of the nineties. He found that property was able to be bought for peanuts then and he carefully started to create his empire which became formidable.

Wilfred never had any looks. His face was angular and his hair was departing regularly every year, and his teeth could not be recommended.

His build and equipment however was adequate and he could satisfy most individuals that came his way. Fourteen years earlier he had met Gloria.

He had telephoned a typing agency for a typist to help him, and a Miss Lamarr had arrived. She typed extremely well, and she liked the circus that was Wilfred's empire. When she arrived for the interview, her cream blouse could scarcely hide her outsized breasts, and her skirt showed a leg that many a chorus girl would envy. She was as blonde as Marilyn Monroe and, altogether, Wilfred thought she was the 'most'.

After the letters had been typed and dispatched, he suggested a drink which was immediately accepted. This led to an invitation that any red-blooded man could hardly refuse. Her clothes came off with a speed that resembled a house fire and she got Wilfred's trousers off in record time. His sexual prowess was first class even if his looks were not. One should not always look at a face when everything downstairs is going like the clappers!

It wasn't long before an association emerged and Gloria saw her chance of promotion in the world via a bloke called Wilfred!

Wilfred introduced Gloria into the business and her looks were a plus, and her sex appeal seduced many a man into the sale of a house.

Wilfred knew that Gloria was no angel, but then angels rarely lived up to their testimonials or expectations.

**

Teddy saw Fay at the supermarket. He hadn't given up on her, in spite of her mother. If Fay was under age so what! Her mother could have made it all up. Fay was still at her usual till and he told himself that she seemed more attractive than ever. He had a quick word as she packed his groceries.

"Same time Friday?" he asked.

"Why not!" Fay nodded.

Teddy smiled and almost patted himself on the back. Fay would be a treat, and so completely different to Gloria, and Martha. He hadn't anything else lined up for Friday and the proposed meeting with Fay excited him. He wondered if they would get to the Lonely Duck pub this time!

Friday came and Teddy waited outside the shop for Fay. When the store closed and Fay emerged, she looked ravishing. She wore her hair up, not down on her shoulders. He took her arm when, suddenly, there stood a woman in middle of their path. It was Daisy, Fay's mother.

"Where do you think you are going?" she enquired, coldly.

"We're just going for a quick drink," replied Fay.

"I think not!" Daisy stated flatly, turning to Teddy. "You haven't learnt your lesson yet, Teddy Jones."

"I don't know what you mean," said Teddy, innocently.

Fay was obviously unaware of the previous meeting between her mother and her escort. She looked a little bewildered.

"What a pity your memory is so short, Teddy," she remarked acidly.

"You're a bit young for dementia."

"We're only planning a drink Mummy!" Fay protested.

"That's a new word for it!" chortled Daisy.

"If I were you, I'd shut up and let Fay have some peace," Teddy growled, "and by the way, your photographs are carefully locked away in my safe."

Daisy glared at Teddy, and realised that she had lost the battle.

"What pictures?" asked Fay innocently.

"None of your business," retorted Daisy. "I expect you home in an hour, lady, and you'd better not be late!"

She glared at Teddy. "I could kill you."

"I don't think that would be wise, Daisy," Teddy laughed. "Funerals don't come cheap these days."

Teddy and Fay strode off, leaving the disgruntled Daisy by the kerbside.

***

Richard often took papers to and from Wilfred and Gloria. Their house was straight across town and not too far from the office, so the little job of investigation was quite simple. He could see that Gloria was in fine form for he knew her well. Perhaps this new employee was responsible.

Richard looked in the office diary and could see that three couples were due to view property in the coming week. Teddy was assigned to all three on various days. Richard would inform Wilfred.

Gloria entered the office.

"Hi, Gloria," Richard greeted her. "I've brought the usual three for signature."

"Fine," said Gloria, kissing him lightly on the cheek. "How's things your end?"

"Good."

"Tell Wilfred. I'll get him up to date when I get home tonight, and tell him that I won't be late."

Richard looked at the 'available' chart on the wall and noticed that the flat next door was not included.

"I thought the flat next door was empty?" he asked.

"Oh, Teddy needed somewhere to stay for a few weeks, so he's in there," Gloria replied quickly.

"Oh!"

"It works quite well," said Gloria.

Richard was sure that it did!

"Is Wilfred in a good mood?" she asked.

"He's a little frustrated," Richard replied. "As you know, he gets these moods of melancholy, so we go out driving when that happens."

"How are you coping with the business?" asked Richard.

"Oh, I'm coping quite well," Gloria declared. "We have a few houses sticking. Could be the time of year, or cash could be short."

"It's quiet all round," Richard said.

There was a knock on the door and Teddy arrived. He shook Richard's hand and there was a touch of electricity as their hands met.

74

"Oh! Hot stuff! Hello! Just came in to get this file," Teddy said, reaching over Richard.

"I've got a two o'clock, and I've got to fly." With that he left the room.

"He's a bit of alright," Richard remarked saucily.

"I bet you wouldn't say no!" replied Gloria.

Richard gathered up the papers for Wilfred. Gloria was never sure about Richard.

"See you later," shouted Teddy as he left the offices.

Richard would have to tell Wilfred, but decided to keep it to himself for a while, after all tomorrow was another day.

***

Aunt Clara was as good as her word and arrived with her bags as planned.

"I couldn't get your uncle to move, Emma, so I've left him up in Yorkshire. You are more important at the moment. I'm afraid you have been totally abused by your brother. He never was any good. Anyway, I'm here to sort everything out."

"Yes, Aunt Clara," said Emma, dragging her suitcases up the stairs.

"You poor girl," Aunt Clara remarked. "Anyway, I'm here now and everything will change. You'll see."

Clara knew she had to pick up the pieces of Emma's life. Her mother, Rose, had been her mainstay and the poor girl did not have a lot upstairs, and would have to be sorted out.

Aunt Clara settled in well. She reorganised the kitchen, redecorated the lounge and did all she could to look after Emma. After several weeks, Teddy paid them a visit. Aunt Clara was not amused.

"What do you want?" she demanded.

"I need some fresh clothes, I left some upstairs."

"I don't know how you have the cheek to pay us a visit after all the turmoil you put Emma through," Aunt Clara glared at him.

Teddy ignored her chattering and spoke to Emma.

"Hi, Emma."

Emma looked at him. He seemed to have aged a lot.

"Hello, Teddy. I've got used to the fact you don't live here anymore."

"We had some good times though, eh?" Teddy grinned at her.

"Yes."

"Some unmentionable times as well, if you ask me!" Aunt Clara snapped.

"Nobody did, Aunt Clara!"

"I could have you shot, young man, for your treachery! Thank God I discovered all your little games before Emma was beyond care."

Teddy pursed his lips. "I was just introducing Emma to life, which was necessary. She had been on her own far too long, and I made her see what life is all about."

"Oh! That's what it was, was it! You had better watch your step Teddy Jones, that's all I'm saying."

Teddy had had more than enough of Clara and went upstairs and threw a handful of clothes into his travelling bag. A few minutes later he came down.

"So long, Emma, we'll catch up again soon," he said. With a vicious look at Aunt Clara, Teddy was gone.

"Good riddance to bad rubbish, that's what I say!" declared Clara.

***

The doorbell rang, and Emma went to answer it. There stood Sam.

"Hello, Emma."

Emma was genuinely pleased to see him.

"Have you brought back my work?" she enquired eagerly.

"Yes, I brought it back as soon as I could," Sam smiled.

Emma showed him into the lounge and Sam carefully put the scrapbook on the table. At that moment, Aunt Clara came in.

"Who is this, Emma?" she demanded.

"It's Sam."

"That tells me nothing!" Aunt Clara snapped. "Emma – do try and be a little more explicit!" She turned to Sam. "Young man! You were not expected."

"I'm sorry Ma'am," Sam apologised. "I should have telephoned to see if it was convenient."

"So you should," Aunt Clara declared. "Manners maketh man, I always say. How long have you known Emma?"

"Not very long, Ma'am," Sam replied. "I'm really here on business."

"Business?" Aunt Clara was surprised.

Emma was suddenly excited. "Oh, Sam, did your boss like my work?"

"Yes, Emma, he did," Sam looked very pleased with himself. "He thought that the designs were exceptional."

"What are we talking about young man?" Aunt Clara interrupted.

"I am talking about Emma's designs," Sam announced.

"Designs?" Aunt Clara asked in puzzlement. Emma opened her scrapbook and displayed her work to Clara.

"What have you to do with this work?" Aunt Clara eyed Sam suspiciously.

"I realised it was worth showing my boss, and it was," Sam was treading the boards carefully.

"Well, what of it!" Aunt Clara demanded. "Where do we go from here?"

"Mr. Butler would like to see Emma on the sixteenth," Sam replied.

"The sixteenth?" Aunt Clara asked. "And for what purpose?"

Sam was getting embarrassed. "It could lead to a commission for Emma, at least I think so."

"Be definite!" Aunt Clara snapped. "How did you come to know Emma?"

Emma jumped in. "He delivered something for Teddy."

"Oh, and what was that?"

"Just a parcel, Ma'am and Emma and I got talking," Sam explained quickly.

"Just talking?" Aunt Clara was digging.

"Just talking!"

Emma started to get upset.

"Alright Emma, don't get upset," Aunt Clara calmed down. "I'll deal with this."

Clara faced Sam. "Your boss's name is?"

"Mr. Butler."

"The firm? The address?"

"Greystones, Design for Business, and we're in First Avenue."

"The day and time of the interview?"

"The sixteenth Ma'am. At twelve noon."

"Your card!"

Sam coloured. Who was this woman? He gave her his card.

Clara looked at it closely.

"Hmmm, seems genuine."

"I can assure you that it is, Ma'am."

"I will telephone to confirm that Emma and I will be there. The sixteenth at noon. That will be all."

Sam gave Emma a withering look, no doubt remembering his sexual awakening and Emma's as well."

"You don't have to go, Sam," Emma whispered. "We could talk."

"I'd like that," Sam declared.

Clara bristled. "I'm going to the kitchen, Emma, I won't be a minute."

With that, she sailed out of the room and shut the door behind her.

"Who was that!" asked Sam.

"My Aunt Clara, she's come to look after me."

"Does she know anything about…you know…"

"Oh! No!" Emma said quickly. "She doesn't know anything. Oh, Sam, I do like you. Quite a lot."

"I'm glad, but I am genuine and I may have done some good for you with my boss."

"Do you think he's into butterflies? I love them. They flutter about in the garden and they seem to multiply a lot in hot weather."

"I think it could be called breeding."

"How very odd," Emma suddenly asked. "Have you done it again Sam? You know – what we did."

"Oh, no," Sam blushed. "No one's asked me."

"I just wanted to know," Emma said. "You don't mind?"

"Of course not," Sam smiled.

Aunt Clara bustled into the room.

"Time's up, Sam," she announced. "We will probably see you when we come to visit Mr. Butler. I will telephone him, but just in case I don't get through to him, you can confirm my visit."

"It's Emma he wants to see Ma'am," Sam declared firmly.

"I will be there as well," Aunt Clara stated. "I will look after Emma and her butterflies. Goodbye, Sam."

"Yes, Ma'am." He hastily made his departure.

"That boy is very young for such an adventure," concluded Aunt Clara.

"I will telephone to see if the appointment is worth the effort. If they want your work, which I doubt, I'll see that you get the going rate! Now, let's say no more about it – Tea!"

Chapter Three

Gloria was in a good mood. She had found Wilfred very pleased with her efforts and she thought things were going so well. She wished she could do more for her husband. Their sex life was no more, but she showed him much affection, which seemed to please Wilfred. She felt for him and her feelings for him were genuine. They had gone together like peaches and cream. What he lacked in looks, he had more than made up for in the bedroom department. He had also taught her to be a strong business woman. His disability would have killed a lesser man but he tried to be cheerful and as busy as he could be.

That very morning, Abigail Appleby had telephoned the office. Gloria liked Abigail. She had bought a flat from them a few years ago, and she now wanted something larger. Her husband had died and had left her a manufacturing company and a fortune. She was a client to be nurtured.

An appointment was arranged for three that afternoon.

Gloria made sure that her make-up was immaculate and that her trouser suit was trendy. Abigail was so rich, so powerful, and she was nobody's fool. Gloria was desperate to impress her by any means in her power. Abigail arrived, looking a million dollars. She wore a designer wrap around skirt and stylish blouse and jacket that showed off every asset of her body. Gloria warmed to her immediately.

"It's great to see you, Abigail," Gloria welcomed her.

"Likewise," Abigail smiled. "Now, have you some mansions to recommend?"

"Of course."

"How is Wilfred?" Abigail asked.

"He copes," Gloria replied, "but he can't do much as you know."

"It's great he's got you in command, running the business."

"I have a personal assistant now," Gloria declared. "Teddy will be helping you."

"Great, let's see him!"

Gloria pressed a bell on her desk and Teddy came into the office.

Abigail eyed him provocatively.

"Pleased to meet you, madam." Teddy gave her a brilliant smile. He didn't miss a trick.

"Likewise," Abigail eyed him from top to toe. "I am sure we will get along famously. Now let's see some photographs."

Gloria, Abigail and Teddy studied over a dozen photographs of some possible mansions.

"I have a lot of entertaining to do as you can imagine," declared Abigail. "I have a certain image to live up to!"

"Don't we know it!" agreed Gloria with a smile.

Abigail selected a mansion that she liked.

"Granville Court. Five bedrooms, three en suite, four reception rooms and large kitchen – that looks like it. When can I inspect?"

Gloria looked at her notes. "Now, today if you have the time."

"Great. Do I get the cowboy?" Abigail smiled at Teddy.

"Of course."

Teddy looked her over. She was really something, but no one's easy meat, he told himself. He thought the 'cowboy' bit was a little daring.

As they left the office, Abigail gave Gloria a knowing wink.

"I'm sure Teddy will look after you," Gloria declared.

***

Wilfred was not in a good mood. Richard could tell that the moment he set eyes on him.

"Not feeling well, Wilfred?" he asked.

Wilfred glared.

"I think not!" Wilfred glared at Richard. "A little bird tells me that Teddy is now in one of my flats next to the office."

Richard didn't know exactly how to play this.

"Really?"

"Yes, really," snapped Wilfred. "I don't think you did your homework, Richard. I don't like this at all. Warn Gloria that I want an explanation."

"I'm sure it is only a temporary arrangement," stated Richard dismissively, anxious to please his employer.

"It had better be," growled Wilfred. "I don't trust this chap at all. There have been no sales for two weeks. I'm not a happy man!"

"A whisky perhaps?" suggested Richard.

Wilfred glared at him. "A large one! I can see I will have to pay a little visit to the office sometime soon, and see what's going on!"

Richard immediately poured Wilfred a large whisky.

"I suppose you'd better have one too, Richard. You're not driving are you?"

"Not today, unless you want me to," Richard replied carefully.

"I'm not sure you deserve one!" Wilfred was in a bad mood. "Listen, Richard, I rely on you to tell me everything."

Richard was a little worried. In no way did he want to upset Wilfred.

"I'll go over first thing in the morning, and see what I can find out."

"I suppose that will have to do. Find out more about this Teddy Jones."

"I believe he is a very good salesman," Richard declared.

"Rather depends on exactly what he is selling, wouldn't you think!"

Wilfred gulped down his whisky.

Richard wondered whether Wilfred was right. He was never certain whether Wilfred trusted Gloria or not. He knew that Wilfred was no longer able to offer the same service that Gloria required. Wilfred obviously thought that Teddy was a sort of gigolo, to whom he was paying a salary! Gloria, in her own way, obviously loved Wilfred, and was grateful for all that he had done for her.

Richard poured another whisky for his employer and the tension eased.

***

Aunt Clara and Emma sat in the Greystone offices. A secretary appeared.

"Do you have an appointment?" she asked.

"I most certainly have!" snapped Clara, "Or I wouldn't be here!"

"Your name, Madam?" The secretary did her best to be polite to this rude woman.

"Clara Sullivan."

"And the young lady?"

"Emma."

"Does she have a surname?"

"Jones. She's here to see Mr. Butler."

"Would you like coffee?" the secretary asked sweetly.

"Certainly not!" snapped Aunt Clara. "Is this Mr. Butler likely to be long? I haven't got all day!"

The secretary bristled. "Neither has Mr. Butler."

At that moment, the office door opened and there stood Julian Butler. He was about thirty-five with large horn rimmed glasses. He wore a white shirt and dark trousers. Clara was impressed. He seemed to know his business.

"Miss Jones?" he enquired.

"I am Mrs. Sullivan. I am here with Emma Jones, and the subject is her work."

"Quite."

Julian Butler ushered them into his office, and closed the door.

"Now, young man, what is your enquiry?" Aunt Clara asked briskly.

Emma started fidgeting and was becoming extremely nervous. She had never been in a situation like this before.

"Hardly an enquiry, Mrs. Sullivan," Julian Butler stated. "I liked Emma's work and we are always on the lookout for talented artists with ideas we can pass on to our clients. Design is our expertise."

"Indeed!" Clara raised her eyebrows. "Has the firm been in business long?"

"Forty years, at least, and currently we have contracts with over twenty suppliers."

"That seems to be encouraging," Aunt Clara conceded grudgingly.

Julian Butler, thought it was high time that he put this dragon in her place.

"I am pleased you think so, Madam. Now, to get down to business and why I have asked to see you, or rather Emma."

"Go on!"

"Oh, I shall," said Julian. Butler spoke directly to Emma. "I was impressed with your work, Emma, and in particular I love the butterfly designs."

Emma started to pay attention.

"Do you really?" She looked so young and so eager.

"That's what I said, and that's what I mean. We have a new soap entering the market and I really feel that the first butterfly design in your book might attract our client. It is colourful, clean cut, and has a touch of fantasy."

"Yes, I like that one too," Emma leant forward. "It has many colours, my butterfly, similar to a rainbow."

"That's one way of describing it, Emma."

Aunt Clara pursed her lips. "And the next step is? If there is to be a next step."

"I would like to put a provisional pencil on this particular design," Julian Butler stated.

"And where does that lead us, young man?"

"I will send the design to my client and see if he likes it."

Clara relaxed a little and nodded to Emma.

"What will be the fee for such an arrangement?" Aunt Clara asked.

Julian Butler gave her a look that would have silenced many a grand dame.

"Five hundred pounds is the norm for an initial proposal," he declared.

Emma jumped up excitedly "Five hundred pounds for my butterfly?"

Aunt Clara glared at Emma. "Be quiet, Emma, or you'll do yourself a mischief!"

Julian Butler leaned forward. "Do we have a deal?"

Clara sat Emma down.

"I take it you represent Emma," Julian Butler asked.

"Precisely," Aunt Clara nodded. "I look forward to a contract and your cheque."

Julian Butler smiled at Emma. "Thank you, Emma. I like your work immensely."

Emma beamed and jumped up and down. "He likes it! Will it be on television?"

"Emma! Be quiet! Do behave!" barked Clara.

Julian Butler suddenly snapped. "I find your manner towards Emma rather severe."

"What you think is really not my concern in this matter," Aunt Clara responded icily. "Please stick to business." She stood up and headed for the door.

"I bid you good day madam," Julian Butler said politely as he opened the door.

He smiled at Emma. "Thank you, Emma, for your design. I am sure we will be writing to you shortly."

He ushered them out and slammed the door.

***

Teddy drove carefully to the mansion known as Granville Court. He was the epitome of politeness, joining in Abigail's conversation as they sped along.

"Have you been working for Gloria long?" Abigail asked.

"Four months."

"Oh!" she said as she touched his knee. "You like the work?"

"Immensely," Teddy's pulse raced.

"Gloria's come a long way in a short time. That girl is going places, mark my words." Abigail looked at Teddy. She could do with someone like him. Her servants were satisfactory, but if you could combine a bit of eye candy with ability, so much the better.

This part of town was attractive. Large flower beds graced the roads, and there were trees everywhere. She noted a railway station nearby – not that she would use it often, but it might be handy. The neighbourhood was privatised, and the road a little set back from the main highway. Teddy parked the car and helped Abigail out. They walked together to the front of a rather imposing mansion. He fitted the key in the lock, and opened the door.

"Welcome to Granville Court," said Teddy.

The hall was impressive, and definitely had the wow factor. It felt lived in rather than a model house on show. After a brief look at downstairs they went upstairs.

The mansion was partially furnished and the decor was pleasing without being ostentatious or dull. Abigail made notes on her iPad and took some photographs.

Teddy also took down every word she said. Eventually, they sat down in the lounge and reviewed Abigail's ideas and remarks.

"I like it, Teddy, if the price is right," she said. "It definitely is a possibility."

It was a warm afternoon, and Teddy was thankful he was not wearing a jacket.

Nothing worse than someone who sweats like a matador.

Abigail spotted a bottle of wine on the bar which occupied the corner of the room.

"I think a glass of wine would do us some good." She checked the label. "Not bad."

Teddy found two glasses and a bottle opener, and poured them both a drink.

"It has some very good points," Abigail declared. "Let's go and look at the garden."

Abigail took off her jacket and threw it at Teddy, revealing her ample breasts through her virtually see-through blouse. Teddy followed her out into the sunshine, carrying her jacket. The grounds were extensive, and she noted that there would be room for a swimming pool. Eventually, they returned indoors.

"I want to see the downstairs bathroom again," Abigail declared.

"Why not!" said Teddy.

The bathroom was, indeed, sumptuous. The bath was a large Jacuzzi one, as was the shower with gold fittings. Dominating the room was a mirrored ceiling.

"I think that bath has room enough for two, possibly three, don't you think? It's such a hot day – why don't we try it out! Are you game?" Abigail asked.

Teddy couldn't believe his luck.

Abigail started to undress and whipped off her cross-over skirt as if it was a matadors cape. For a late fortyish lady, she was very well upholstered.

"Come on, Teddy, don't take all day," she chided.

In a flash, Teddy's boots were off, his trousers were around his ankles, and Abigail had yanked his shirt off brutally. His pecs were well defined on his gorgeous body. He stood there in his briefs waiting for Abigail to take hers off.

Teddy turned on the water and Abigail tested its warmth and turned on the motor.

"Even the soap is a good make," she declared. "Well, get in, Teddy."

Teddy whipped off his briefs and there he stood in all his glory. Abigail was delighted. She hadn't seen anything so interesting, or so big, for some time! She started to soap his front with comforting hands and his equipment became larger by the minute. He mused that it obviously liked the soap.

"Turn around," demanded Abigail. "Your butt needs a little attention."

He did as she said and soon her hands were caressing his back and the contours of his bum, soaping him all over while kissing him feverishly on the lips. Eventually, they both lay down in the spacious bath and adored the warmth of the water as it whirled around their bodies. She looked up at the ceiling mirror and delighted in the sight of Teddy's magnificent backside bobbing in and out of the swirling soap bubbles as she had the ride of her life. After ten minutes or so their sexual appetites were satisfied, and they lay back in the caressing water to catch their breath.

"Well, that was a bonus, and no mistake!" said Abigail. "The fact that you are built like a stallion, Teddy, makes all the difference."

After a while, they got out of the bath and he dried her down with a large fluffy towel.

"That was good, Teddy. Quite exciting," Abigail said.

Teddy was drained. He had put quite a bit of effort into pleasing Abigail.

She took it all in her stride. 'Strong as a pig' thought Teddy – but very dainty with it.

Abigail decided that the inspection of Granville Court and the man was a good afternoon's work and that that was enough. She would pay Gloria a visit in a day or two. She had plans both for her purchase of the mansion, and for Teddy, but it could all wait for another day.

***

Julian Butler was sure he was onto a winner with Emma's butterfly design and he felt that Sam should get a small bonus if it happened. Sam was an adopted child. His parents had been killed in an accident and he had been adopted by Rosemary and her husband Grant. They were a childless couple.

They had tried several times, and were more than happy when they managed to adopt Sam. They were loving parents and schooled him well. He didn't make college but that didn't upset them or Sam. Grant was an engineer and Rosemary was a school teacher, and the three of them made a most agreeable family.

Sam was always a nervous child, and not sure about the future. He was a lonely boy in spite of his loving upbringing, and was very insecure about his sexuality which is why he paid a visit to Emma in the first place.

Julian Butler was a friend of Rosemary's and, when the time came for Sam to pursue a career, Julian promptly offered him a junior position in his firm. Sam had intelligence, liked his job and the firm. Julian liked Sam and believed he would go far. Sam couldn't have had a better mentor.

Sam had met Teddy in a pub where Teddy was scouting for customers to take advantage of his sister. Sam was concerned about his stupidity where sex was concerned and decided, after a drink or two, to pay Emma a visit.

He couldn't quite make Teddy out but decided to go along for the ride. He didn't like being a virgin and Teddy seemed to have the answer. That was how Sam discovered Emma who was like a breath of spring. His interest in her and his affection for her had grown as time went by. He had discovered his masculinity and now he had introduced her to his world at Greystone.

Chapter Four

Abigail was taken with Granville Court. It was just the size she needed and, as a bonus, she was more than taken with Teddy Jones and the size he offered. Not only was he stacked, but she was sure that he could satisfy her every desire in the bedroom.

Their episode in the bathroom was a suitable trailer for triumphs to come. Abigail called on Gloria Trent to negotiate the deal. She did wonder if Teddy had mentioned the bathing episode, but Gloria wasn't giving anything away.

"Gloria, I'm going to take Granville Court," Abigail announced. "It seems to be just what I am looking for, but no overcharging, if you please. I'm not made of money!"

Gloria looked her up and down. "Shall we start at two and a half? I know that's the tag that Wilfred has on it."

"No, that's not on," protested Abigail. "I'll give you two million and I want to borrow Teddy to help me finish the job. Well, what do you say?"

Gloria looked down her nose a little, but Abigail had made up her mind.

"I'll have to speak to Wilfred," she declared. "It's a large property and we do have others interested."

Abigail pulled a face "It's a large offer. There are no others interested, and you have had it empty for seven months. I checked."

Gloria smiled to herself. Abigail certainly didn't miss a trick and she concluded that that was why she was so wealthy.

"Get back to me tomorrow," ordered Abigail, and don't forget that the arrangement includes Teddy for a month!"

"Of course!" Gloria nodded. "We will agree to that!"

Abigail smiled. When she had finished with Teddy, he wouldn't want to return to Gloria. She would make sure of that! She didn't want Teddy to put his equipment anywhere else – well not for a while anyway.

***

Gloria arrived home early and, as the day was very warm, Richard was sun bathing on the terrace with his top off. His hot muscles gleamed in the sun and Gloria's mouth became dry as she imagined her lips on those sturdy nipples.

Wilfred was waiting for her. She had telephoned him earlier reporting her conversation with Abigail.

"You have done well, Gloria?" Wilfred asked.

"Not yet," Gloria said. "She's only come up with two million."

"Not really enough," Wilfred frowned.

"Well, we have had Granville Court up for sale over seven months," Gloria said.

"True, but I'm in no mood to give half a million away to that tart!" Wilfred declared vehemently.

Gloria poured herself a drink and one for Wilfred. She always thought that liquor was helpful when sorting things out.

"I trust you've got that gigolo, Teddy, out of my flat by now!" Wilfred gave her a knowing eye. "He may be a good salesman, but I wouldn't trust him further than I could throw him."

"That wouldn't be very far would it?" Gloria replied cheekily. They laughed. "I see Richard is toning up his body," said Gloria looking out of the window.

"It's good to have an Adonis about the house!" Wilfred said.

Gloria gave Wilfred a look that spoke reams. It was exactly what she was thinking.

"I'll have to think about Granville Court," said Wilfred.

"Abigail wants to know by four o'clock tomorrow, and she wants Teddy thrown in as well!" Gloria stated.

"For how long?"

"She said a month! To help her sort everything out, she said."

Wilfred laughed. "Is she on fire or something? I'll think about it!"

"I think I'll go and change, I've been in this all day," Gloria said as she left the room. Across the hallway was a small room which she often used as a bedroom. Richard passed the window as she discarded her skirt and started to pull on a smart pair of slacks. The door opened and Richard appeared.

"Nice to see you Gloria."

"Likewise." She moved quickly over to him and ran her fingers over his glistening chest. She then slid her hand down to his crotch, which seemed to be growing.

"Hmmm, nice!" she said as she squeezed a little. "But – another time. At the moment I have to see to Wilfred."

"Of course," said Richard as he patted her dainty rear. "Have you negotiated a good deal on Granville Court?"

95

"It could be ok if Wilfred makes up his mind," Gloria said as she left the room. Richard laughed, tomorrow was another day.

***

Aunt Clara was as good as her word. She had arrived with a small suitcase and had organised Emma, right, left and centre. The funny thing was, that Emma responded to her regime and had started to plot her day to help Aunt Clara with the cooking and the cleaning. Emma was generally growing up a little.

The doorbell rang and Aunt Clara went to answer it. A tall, dark, moustached man around forty stood on the doorstep.

"Are you the lady of the house?" he began.

"Well, I'm not Snow White if that's what you mean! I'm not expecting any visitors."

"Oh, I'm not just any visitor. I am enquiring about a certain Teddy Jones. Is he in?"

Aunt Clara was, as always, abrupt and to the point.

"Certainly not!"

"He does live here?"

"No! He doesn't," she said coldly as she looked at his sombre clothing, "and I have no idea where he is. I also do not wish to know."

Emma ventured out of the kitchen to see who it was.

"I can't stand here all day answering your questions!" Aunt Clara declared.

The man stiffened. He did not like her tone.

"Is Teddy a relation?"

"Regrettably, yes!" snapped Aunt Clara.

Emma came forward. "Teddy? He's my brother."

"Thank you, Miss. Now we're getting somewhere."

"Oh, no you're not! We don't know where Teddy Jones is, and we don't want to know. Good day to you," Aunt Clara declared as she slammed the door in his face.

Emma looked enquiringly at Aunt Clara. "I know where he is! I sent him a letter!"

"Where he WAS, Emma – and you shouldn't communicate with him. Rascals like your brother never stay anywhere long. Take my word for it, he probably owes money or is involved in something criminal."

They withdrew into the lounge.

"Do you think Teddy's in trouble?"

"Most probably, but not as much as if he came round here! Now, Emma, we have things to do. Time waits for no man, my child."

Emma paused. "I'm hardly a child, Auntie."

"Oh! We're grown up all of a sudden are we?" Aunt Clara raised her eyebrows.

"Wonders will never cease!"

"Do you think he was a policeman?" Emma asked.

"He could possibly be a policeman in plain clothes. But more likely it's a bill that's not been paid. Now, don't worry your head about such things. I am more interested in what Julian Butler comes up with. Now that's a most interesting situation!" Aunt Clara turned on the television and left the room to make herself a cup of tea in the kitchen. Emma sat down with her thoughts.

***

The sale of Granville Court went ahead and Abigail bought it for the two million plus Teddy. A week later, she started organising and furnishing the house and Teddy started his month with Abigail. Teddy had done some research on the mansion for Abigail, that included some decorating and he suggested that she got someone in to keep the garden in order.

This was not a bad idea as it was rather large and Abigail had no interest in gardening.

Teddy was a great help to Gloria in more ways than one. She asked if he was still living in the flat next door to Gloria's office. He confirmed that he was which gave Abigail food for thought.

"I think you could stay upstairs in one of the guest bedrooms while you are helping me," she suggested.

Teddy immediately leapt on the idea.

"Good," said Abigail. "Shall we get on?"

Furniture and pictures started arriving and Teddy was dazzled by the amount of money that Abigail was splashing around. Abigail, although sexually aroused by her new assistant, kept her distance as the days went by.

She salivated about the episode in the bath, and promised herself that she would probably help herself to his goods at the end of the first week.

Gloria missed Teddy in more ways than one, but at least it got her off the leash with Wilfred and the flat, which he told her to sell immediately.

***

Richard was delighted to tell Wilfred of Teddy's temporary departure.

If he could, Wilfred would make sure that the flat was not available when or if he returned. He was getting increasingly irritable about his disability. His world was too minimal. He needed a new avenue to explore, to enthuse about, to speculate and release his frustrations upon. Richard noted this and decided he would keep a look out for a suitable venture.

Wilfred, after all, was a rich man. He was into stocks and shares continually and Richard could see some gold at the end of the rainbow.

***

Gloria was missing the availability of Teddy's sexual services. It did not please her one little bit. It was not too much of a surprise when she cornered Richard when he picked up the mail and suggested that a roll in the hay might not be a bad thing. Richard lapped up the idea. What was the use of having the machinery and no opportunity to show off his prowess.

Gloria took him in every way. He was a dish and could operate like a machine gun. He sent Gloria into screams of passion and delight, and for a time, she forgot all about Teddy and his slightly larger manhood. She couldn't make up her mind if she should look for another salesman for the business. She had only loaned Teddy to Abigail for a month, but she was not foolish enough to pretend that he might not want to return to her after the agreed period. She still had Richard who could satisfy her needs.

Gloria and Wilfred knew that a salesman to show clients around properties was necessary. He would have to be good looking, sharp and young. They would be on the lookout for such a person.

***

Alice saw quite a bit of Aunt Clara, who had turned the house, and Emma upside down. She had renovated, altered and re-upholstered everything.

Emma was changing slowly and getting a new perspective on life. After all she would have five hundred pounds in the bank that she had earned, and a young man called Sam as her friend.

Alice was astounded with the changes both in the house and in Emma.

She had got on well with Clara, agreeing with all the changes Clara had decreed. She knew that that was the best way to deal with Clara! Six weeks had gone by and Clara knew that she had to go home eventually.

After all, she had a husband and no man would stay adoring unless the icing was renewed on the confection known as marriage.

Teddy had not been near them, which was just as well. Clara had spies in the town, and she noted his movements. Alice was attentive. She had time on her hands and was fond of Emma which was helpful.

Clara noted all this with satisfaction.

***

Things were going well at Granville Court. It was geared for social gatherings as intended and Teddy fulfilled every demand that Abigail expected. She spoke to Gloria and said she would like Teddy to stay on a little longer. Gloria was not surprised and was already planning on a replacement. Teddy, meanwhile, was enjoying life at Granville Court. The pool was finally to be installed and now a gardener had to be found to tend the large garden. Abigail had a friend who ran an agency. She seemed to have friends everywhere. Muriel, who ran the agency, came up with two possible gardeners. There were two male gardeners and one female, which was a novelty in itself.

The first gardener was aged sixty-five if he was a day. He was very experienced, but he appeared so ancient, and there was a possibility that he would conk out before the harvest festival!

The second one was more like it. He was tall, bronzed, dark-haired and sturdy. He also appeared to be well stacked which pleased Abigail.

He went by the name of Gregory – his mother must have been in love with Gregory Peck. When he sat down, his legs were widely spread and Abigail could imagine the goods that the corduroy trousers sported.

He seemed to be made for love, and Abigail liked variety.

Gregory was invited to have a drink in the afternoon. Abigail, to make sure the coast was clear, sent Teddy off to the gym for the afternoon. Abigail had set the scene well.

The telephone was off the hook, and her blouse was so low cut that her ample breasts almost fell out. One drink led to another and, after the fourth drink, he quickly threw off his clothes and performed as nature intended. His technique was superb and delivery very satisfactory.

"Shall we talk business, Gregory?" said Abigail when she had recovered her composure, and adjusted her dress.

"What a good idea!" he said as he climbed back into his trousers.

"I think you would be fine to look after my various flower beds."

'Other beds as well', thought Gregory, tucking in his shirt.

"When could you start?" Abigail enquired.

"It depends on the deal," Gregory declared.

"Six hundred pounds a week, how does that feel?" Abigail asked.

"It's a start, I suppose."

Abigail raised an eyebrow.

"You have references, I presume?" she asked.

"Why?" Gregory was surprised.

"My husband would want to see them."

"You have a husband?" Gregory was shocked.

"Doesn't everyone?" Abigail laughed.

Gregory suddenly changed colour.

"I need time to consider," he stammered. "I do have other offers, and of course there would be extras."

Other offers! Extras! Abigail was stunned. The audacity! A quick fuck was inclusive. She was not going to pay for it! Who did this man think he was, for God's sake?

Abigail sat bolt upright and crossed her legs. "I'll ring the agency in the morning," she said coldly. "Muriel and I are old friends. Shall we leave it at that?"

"Certainly, in the morning!" Gregory nodded awkwardly and withdrew.

"That's punctured his balloon!" Abigail thought.

***

Clara was deep in thought. She had to consider her own husband. He was a gentle creature. He didn't want to leave his home town and his work there. For once he had disagreed with his dominant wife, Clara. He loved the woman, a strong Christian female. He always had done and always would. However, he did not want to move south, and it was decided that Clara would go and look after Emma for a little while. Clara was worried that she couldn't permanently look after Emma.

The child had been through a lot with the loss of her mother, and the fact that she was a little backward worried Clara to the extreme. Perhaps Alice next door was the answer. Clara was not sure.

She still couldn't believe Teddy's treatment of his sister. He was an unscrupulous human being and she couldn't believe that her sister, Rose, could have produced such a low life. She had never really connected with Emma. She was an odd girl at the best of times and her casual education didn't help. She felt that the introduction to Sam and the interest he was showing towards Emma was a step in the right direction. Clara did have her doubts about whether the commission of Emma's work would lead to anything, but when the cheque for five hundred pounds arrived, she admitted to herself that pigs might fly!

When the large cheque arrived, Emma was as excited as if she had won the lottery. She took the cheque in her hands and danced around the room like a mad thing.

"You'd better let me handle this," declared Clara, but Emma stamped her feet and screamed. "No, no, no! It's mine! And the butterflies are mine! Mine, from my own design!"

Clara cleared her throat. "Emma. Let's have no tantrums. I will open a bank account for you and deposit your cheque. No one can draw on it, it is yours and yours alone. It will be your very own bank account. You remember Mr. Julian Butler?"

Emma laughed "Yes, he had a spotted tie."

"Yes. Now if anything else comes from the interview and your designs, I will handle it for you, and see that your interests are observed."

Emma paused. "Will they want any more?"

"They might, and then they might not!" Aunt Clara said. "It depends on which way the wind blows, if you know what I mean."

It was obvious that Emma didn't, but she was beside herself with joy and as excited as she had ever been.

"It's a case of wait and see, Emma," Aunt Clara said.

"Will I see Sam again?" Emma asked.

"If you want to," replied Aunt Clara. "I will arrange it, as obviously the boy could be good news."

***

Time passed and Aunt Clara had to return home to her husband and so it was arranged that Alice would keep an eye on Emma. Emma was maturing and the task would be much easier, and she spent much time on her designs and new drawings. She was beginning to take note of the different designs for different products on the television, and in the papers and magazines.

One morning, Sam arrived. He was in a new suit, fashionable tie, and looked a very handsome young man.

"May I come in, Emma?" he asked.

"Of course!" Emma had a real affection for this young man who was now so much more confident than when they first met. "Would you like some tea?" she asked.

"If it's not too much trouble." Sam sat down on the divan. He seemed distracted and was clearly thinking about something else. Emma made the tea and took it into the sitting room.

"You don't want to." She paused. "You know what? I won't tell Teddy, so you won't have to pay."

Sam coughed nervously.

"Oh, no." Sam leant over and kissed her tenderly on the cheek. "You and I had something special. Neither of us are virgins anymore."

She looked at him affectionately.

"You've forgotten to stir your tea, and you haven't tried the biscuits. They are very good you know." They exchanged smiles.

"Thank you, Emma." He squeezed her hand and started to enjoy his visit.

"Aunt Clara?"

"Up North! Do you know, Sam, I like being on my own. Is that natural?"

He looked at this pretty young woman, so pretty and so gullible. He liked her more and more and perhaps, one day, he could offer to take her out.

That is – when Aunt Clara was not there!

"Have you done any more designs?" he asked.

"Yes, as a matter of fact I have," Emma's eyes lit up. "Would you like to see them?"

"Of course I would."

Emma got out her large drawing pad and the two of them sat there on the divan exploring the pages.

"Yoo Hoo it's me!" The door opened and Alice entered.

"Well! A surprise visitor for you, Emma," she exclaimed. "This is nice. You are Sam. I remember meeting you before and you are responsible for selling Emma's butterfly."

"That's right," said Sam. "And she's done some more, look."

The three of them reviewed Emma's work with enthusiasm. Alice looked at Sam. He was so like the young man she wished she could have borne for her husband. Life was sometimes cruel, and sometimes unexpected in its decisions. Sam coughed and dropped his biscuit in his tea.

"I really came round to tell Emma a little news," he said.

"Yes?" Alice and Emma shared a little excitement.

"I think our client might be going to use Emma's butterfly design," he declared.

Emma was so excited and Alice kissed Sam on the cheek.

"Sam, you really are the tonic Emma needs," Alice exclaimed.

"Well, nothing is certain, but our committee meets next week and they wouldn't be doing that if there wasn't something positive."

Suddenly the door burst open, and there was Teddy!

"She's not here, is she Emma?" he asked quickly.

"Aunt Clara?"

"Of course, where is the old witch?"

"Gone home."

Teddy sat down thankfully next to Sam.

"Now, Sam, it is Sam, isn't it?" he began.

"Yes."

"Any developments with Emma's work, I must handle, do you understand?" Teddy stated.

"But Aunt Clara…" blurted out Alice.

"She has got nothing to do with it! The old bat isn't here, and someone has got to look after Emma's interests."

Alice was concerned. How had Teddy got on to this?

Emma looked flustered. She had to admit she had sent a letter to Teddy telling him of her success.

"You see, Sam, I own this house with Emma, so it's only natural that I should take care of her interests. Now, let's go over the situation."

Sam and Teddy talked. Teddy grinned, this was getting better every minute. Who would have thought that his backward sister could be on to something big! He took Sam's number, filled a suitcase with clothes and bade them good day. He went as suddenly as he arrived.

Alice was worried. This was a turn up for the books. Should she tell Aunt Clara? That was the ten million dollar question!

***

Abigail was still interviewing gardeners when Wendy arrived. She liked her from the start. Wendy knew her gardening, she knew her business, and, with Abigail, she knew that she was on to a good thing.

The money was good, and she liked definite women, and Abigail was certainly most definite. Teddy was paying her attention and as she appreciated a pleasing young man, it wasn't only the flower garden that generated her interest.

A week or two passed and Wendy was doing a splendid job. The lawns were immaculate, the fruit trees were abundant, and the flower beds a joy.

The orchard was at the bottom of the garden and Teddy caught up with Wendy.

"Hello," said Wendy. "I haven't seen you around so much."

"I do have work to do," Teddy noted her tall, slim frame, her red hair that gleamed in the sun and her breasts that helped to make her overall look delicious. The morning was quiet and the weather hot.

"Do you like your work?" he enquired.

"I wouldn't be here if I didn't." She smiled and the sunshine seemed brighter.

Teddy thought that this was an experienced young woman who had to be popular with the boys. He wondered whether she would let him have a try!

He ran his fingers through her flowing locks and put his arm around her waist. She smiled as she felt her body rising to the smell of this rampant young stud. Teddy picked her up effortlessly and put her gently down on the grass. He undid her overalls and her flimsy blouse and fondled her breasts.

His lips kissed her erect nipples and then they gradually moved down her slim body. His manhood reached its full extension and it was ready to burst through his trousers. He released it with ease and slowly he started to make love to this beautiful Titian haired beauty.

Passion took over and the rhythm of his body almost shook the apples off the trees. He came, violently and noisily. Then a shadow fell across the scene.

It was Abigail!

"Get up!" Her command would have done justice to an army sergeant.

Wendy struggled to fasten her overalls and Teddy attempted to put on his trousers. Wendy looked flustered. "I'm sorry," she said.

"So am I!" Abigail took on the appearance of the wicked witch in the 'Wizard of Oz'. She didn't need a black costume to illustrate her venom. She gestured to Wendy. "Go and water your plants instead of draining this young cowboy!"

Wendy quickly retreated. Abigail felt a little forgiveness within her rage.

The girl had only tasted the wine that so recently had reached her own lips.

She turned to Teddy. "Now hear this, sunny boy. I do not accept double dealings from you especially when I pay you six hundred pounds a week.

You have overstepped the mark this time. You don't service the gardener when your mistress is away. Do it again and I will destroy you, puncture your equipment and finish you off, if you are not very careful!"

Teddy smiled gently pouring on his charm to relieve the situation.

"It was only a kiss that got out of hand," he pleaded.

"Ha! A likely tale," Abigail snorted. "This is not the Garden Of Eden. Gather up your things and take your equipment back to Gloria Trent who, no doubt, will open her legs willingly!"

"Abigail..."

"Goodbye, Teddy Jones," Abigail called back firmly as she swept up the lawn towards the house.

***

Chapter Five

Julian Butler had negotiated a deal for Emma's butterfly design. It was a new product destined to be released to the population with speed. It would have a full advertising campaign which would include television adverts, magazines, and newspapers. Sam was over the moon with excitement. He had been right. Emma did have talent and he had been able to recognise it and, through his introduction, a deal had been made with Greystones. Julian was an honourable man, and he made sure that Sam received a little commission for his suggestion.

Julian rang Clara to say that the company was willing to pay twenty-five thousand for the initial payment, spread over five years, for the design.

This was to include television advertisements for a year with options for worldwide coverage. Clara agreed and Julian would arrange the payments into Emma's new account. She would make sure that Teddy didn't get his grubby little hands on it.

***

Frazer Lloyd had gone to drama school and had emerged with honours.

He had had great luck landing a small part in a West End play. The casting director, Sonia Miller, happened to catch the play. She was a woman in her late forties going on sixty and she knew everything about casting.

She saw a future for young Frazer Lloyd and she was right. She took him under her wing. Frazer was off to a flying start. Whether he extended his other talents to Sonia Miller was unknown. After all, even casting directors have appetites. She recommended him mainly for television commercials, and she was right. Frazer took it on as if he was on fire. Commercial after commercial made him a household name. He was the flavour of the year and his salary rocketed. Then, after several years, his career seemed to slide downhill. On top of that, Sonia developed cancer which put an end to her career, and her expertise in guiding Frazer. Unfortunately, he didn't get the opportunities any more. One thing he knew however, was that he could write.

Two short stories he had penned had already been snapped up by a magazine, and he was already building a second career which could earn him gold pieces. His fervour towards being an actor was beginning to fade. His good looks matured, and he was still a God with matinee idol's looks. He was quite aware that talent and luck went hand in hand in the world of entertainment, and he was ready for whatever came his way.

This turned out to be Emma. When Frazer heard of Emma and her forced services for lonely gentlemen, he realised that here was a story. If properly written it could interest millions. He had been busy devising his story, but he needed more detail, more depth that only Emma could give him. He really liked Emma and he hoped he could bring some colour into her sombre life.

His loathing of Teddy and what he had done to Emma was intense, and if he could get at him for his treachery he would. He rang Emma's number and Alice answered.

"Could I speak to Emma please?" he asked.

"For what reason?" Alice was careful. Clara had left her in charge of Emma.

"She's a friend of mine!" Frazer exuded charm.

"And your name?" Alice enquired guardedly.

"Frazer Lloyd."

Alice nearly had a seizure. Frazer Lloyd the TV star? Alice almost dropped the telephone in her excitement.

"And you are?" Frazer asked politely.

"Alice – Alice Blake," Alice answered breathlessly. "I am looking after Emma while her Aunt Clara is up north."

"Would it be all right if I came over to take her out to dinner tomorrow?" asked Frazer.

"Just a minute. I'll ask." Alice quickly called Emma over, whispering loudly with her hand over the receiver.

"Frazer Lloyd wants to come over and take you out to dinner tomorrow night!" Emma was stunned.

"Do you know this actor?" Alice asked. "He said he was a friend of yours."

Emma trembled. She didn't know how to handle this. Alice took her hand.

"Perhaps you don't want to see him. But it's Frazer Lloyd from the television!" said Alice full of excitement.

"I remember him." Emma suddenly remembered the tall, strange blonde man.

"Yes, I can see him tomorrow."

Alice beamed and spoke into the receiver. "Yes. Tomorrow. Shall we say six o'clock?"

"Perfect." Frazer Lloyd was pleased. "I'll be there at six, and I'll take her out to dinner."

Alice was delighted. She put the phone down and turned to Emma.

"Is there anything you want to tell me?"

"He's a friend of Teddy's." Emma tried to remember. "He brought me a message and we talked."

"What about?" asked Alice.

"Oh, nothing," answered Emma vaguely. "We just said hello!"

"Well, he's coming here at six o'clock tomorrow, and he's taking you out for dinner. You will remember won't you?" Alice fussed.

"I won't forget," Emma promised.

"I must go. I'll pop in later." Alice left in wonderment. The handsome Frazer Lloyd was coming to see Emma! She must make sure that she was there to see him in person at six the following day!

***

Teddy returned to Gloria with his tail between his legs. Abigail was as good as her word, and had swiftly kicked him out. He just hoped that Wendy's garden expertise would be recognised and her indiscretion forgotten, and forgiven.

Abigail was not a forgiving person.

Gloria was delighted to have Teddy back. She had missed him as her salesman, and she had missed him for other reasons too.

"I didn't expect you back so soon!" she said.

"I didn't want to stay away any longer," Teddy said. "Abigail demands too much!"

Gloria grinned to herself. She had no doubts about Abigail and what her demands would be."

"Flat still empty?" enquired Teddy hopefully.

113

"As a matter of fact it is," Gloria smiled.

"Mind if I make myself at home again?" Teddy asked carefully, Gloria was not too sure about this. There was Wilfred to deal with.

"Only a couple of weeks mind, and if the flat is sold, out you go!" Any longer than a couple of weeks and she would have questions to answer.

Teddy smiled triumphantly. Gloria would be richly rewarded the next time that they entwined. He'd make sure it was a bumper one for Miss Gloria!

After all one good turn deserved another!

***

Alice Blake had loved her husband Joe from the moment he swept her off her feet at seventeen years of age. She had been brought up in a strong Church of England home. Her mother hadn't really wished for a child and soon after Alice had arrived, her father took off with a widow on the other side of town.

He had no time for religion. He was a handsome man but didn't like being under a 'contract'. Marriage was not for him, so he looked elsewhere.

The widow was rampant, and with a comfortable income, and he fancied a change.

Alice had always been religious and attended church several times a week.

She, in her way, was a little more than fond of the vicar and fussed over him like a mother hen. Her world was shattered when she found out that the vicar had a boyfriend who was far more attentive. In other words, he was as gay as a kite! This shook her to the core and for several weeks, she stayed away from the church and the vicar while she re-evaluated everything. As she always gave generously to the collection bowl, that didn't do anything for the church funds either.

Joe, who was a bookies clerk, viewed Alice from afar. She was reasonably good looking, dressed well, and had a slim figure. He was looking for a wife and a home. Around this time, Alice's mother passed away and Alice felt very lonely.

They met and the attraction was instant. Alice was not experienced in the ways of the flesh. Her reading matter up until then had consisted of the Christian Herald, and the Church Times.

Then, one autumn day, Joe proposed and she accepted immediately. A small wedding ceremony followed and the vicar officiated. Perhaps this was not a good idea as he was the one who had figured so heavily in her dreams up till then. Alice was not a worshipper in any other church in the town, so she didn't have a choice.

Joe was not an unreasonable man and he loved and tried his best with Alice.

Sex really was not a delight and it gradually took a back seat. She let him have his way once a month.

***

Teddy reviewed his life suddenly. He was making a few quid with Gloria, and he had enjoyed some marvellous shags en route. After all, variety was supposed to be the spice of life. He took stock. He was good looking, tall, and he had a big cock and he liked to use it. Somehow, he had to get his paws on real money, and get somewhere in life. Aunt Clara was forever looking after Emma, so his plans to sell his mother's house were thwarted.

At least, he thought, for the time being. His conquests so far had been enjoyable but contributed fuck all to his bank balance. Women were good news, both for his sexual appetite, and pleasure. However commitment on a long term basis was not his cup of tea.

Grantcombe was a sleepy town where nothing went on to stimulate anyone. The day the local cinema caught fire was the only real excitement for many a long day. Shops that had been there for ages were gradually disappearing and large supermarkets were arriving, cutting out the small tradesmen. The British Legion Hall had already been turned into a casino and the old town hall gardens were a parking lot. It now only had one gym, which he used frequently.

Teddy's thoughts turned to the big city. If he wanted to make real money, he had to go to the big city. He made a resolution that it would be his next port of call.

***

Frazer Lloyd arrived at Emma's on the dot with a bouquet of flowers. Alice made sure that she was there to greet him, and even wore a new apron for the occasion. She liked him on sight, and could remember him from his frequent appearances on television.

"Hello, Emma. These are for you," Frazer said, handing her the flowers. He turned to Alice. "If I had known two ladies were going to be here, I would have brought two bouquets of flowers." Alice blushed profusely.

Frazer, more and more, was relishing his talents as a writer. He knew, inwardly, that he would never make a good actor or a big star. However, there were other conquests worth pursuing, and that was where Emma came in.

Alice was enchanted, there were no two ways about it. The man was as handsome as his fame. He was not at all grand and his voice was electric. Alice was totally enamoured. She had dressed Emma in a lovely dress from her own wardrobe, both being size eight, and Emma's top coat would at least pass muster.

"I have my car outside," Frazer declared. "Shall we go, Emma?"

Emma smiled and nodded. It was something akin to Cinderella going to the ball.

Alice thanked Frazer for his kindness and when she saw the magnificent Mercedes outside. She nearly fainted. It was car for a Princess.

"I'll have her back by nine," promised Frazer. "Will that be acceptable?"

Alice smiled. The man was a gentleman. She waved them off and returned to her house, dazzled by the turn of events.

"Who would have thought it!" she told herself.

***

Teddy had a busy day back at the office and some interesting clients to view the properties.

"For God's sake get a sale, Teddy," Gloria begged as she gave him the necessary notes. "We haven't had a sale for over two weeks. You get one and you'll be handsomely rewarded." She winked and her body reverberated with promise.

The first couple were routine and Teddy doubted whether they had the necessary funds, but the second couple were more like it. Len was from a large company, plump, sandy haired and hitting fifty.

His betrothed was a model. She liked Teddy from the start, assessing his many assets, especially in the lower regions. His eyes practically fell out when he saw her. She was beautiful, alluring, and she had the advantage of promise in her eyes. What she saw in Len, only God knew, but it was plain he was going to have a job on his hands with this attractive female. Teddy felt an urge in his loins and desire coming to the surface. My word she was a dish, but the meal proved to be quite some time away.

***

Emma could not believe that her mother had been dead a year. Time moves so fast, like an express train, she thought. Memories of those you have loved, linger on, and scenes and situations that remind you of them happen frequently.

She missed her mother.

The dinner with Frazer had been a trip into another world. The menu was fascinating, the diners even more so. Frazer was madly attentive and chose dishes for Emma, who was at a loss to know what to choose.

This high class cuisine was something else! There were names and dishes from another world which Emma just did not understand. It was not only the food that caught her attention; the well attired diners and the waiters in their tails were mesmerising.

Emma had started growing up a little, and her mind seemed to be improving.

She was more aware of her own body, something that Teddy had no doubt helped enormously. She still could not forget that Frazer had spurned her body, although his kisses lingered still. He sat opposite her, superbly dressed in a beautiful checked jacket. He wore a light green shirt with a shaded coloured tie to match and dark green trousers.

The waiters fussed around and seemed to know Frazer and greeted him like an old friend. Emma had taken all this in. It was a new world to her and she didn't want to miss a thing. She would be able to report the whole evening to Alice and would telephone Aunt Clara tomorrow. She thought she might not mention the menu to Aunt Clara. That was not a good idea!

The meal went without a hitch, and, when the dessert came, Emma was in seventh heaven. There was a delicious mousse with a raspberry base flooded with cream, while Frazer had ice cream with a selection of fruits to keep it company. Emma just prayed that the evening would never end. She noted that Frazer had a little pad with him on which he wrote notes as the evening progressed. She would have to tell Sam all about this adventure when she next saw him. He would be interested no doubt, as he was the key to Emma's outside world.

She noticed the design on the napkin, a plate surmounted by a rainbow.

She wondered what it might signify. Her brain would have to think this one out!

**

Gloria had an appointment with the bank manager and so left Teddy in charge of the office. Richard arrived with some papers for Gloria. He was well turned out in a dark pink jacket and white shirt which was open at the neck. Teddy took it all in and started to imagine that body without the pink jacket, shirt and pants. He was feeling particularly randy that day and his body became excited at the vision in front of him. He hoped that Richard had not noticed the sudden bulge in his trousers.

"I've got some important papers for Gloria, Teddy." Richard announced.

"She's not here, but you are welcome to come in and wait," Teddy said.

Richard sat down and sprawled his body suggestively on the Chesterfield.

"Wilfred is not your greatest ally, you know. He knows you are back in the flat next door after your episode with Abigail."

"You know Abigail?" Teddy frowned.

"Doesn't everyone?" Richard chuckled. He proffered the papers to Teddy.

"These are new acquisitions and need to be released on the market shortly. Wilfred did well with the buying price and now Gloria will delegate you to sell the flats in the building."

Teddy stood in front of Richard and the bulge in his trousers was very noticeable. He smiled as he noticed Richards eyes wander over his crotch.

"I've often wondered why you haven't moved on," said Teddy with a raised eyebrow.

"Oh, plenty of time for that, and from what I've heard, I've got a lot to learn from you," Richard replied.

"You're too kind," said Teddy, sitting beside him and suddenly kissing him strongly on the lips. Richard responded readily, and they ended up in a passionate embrace. "Come on, the flat's next door," said Teddy.

He dragged Richard up by the belt and headed for the door. In the outer office, Miss West, the elderly secretary, sat at her computer.

"We're going to view the flat next door for Wilfred. We won't be long."

"Very well, Teddy," Miss West said and went back to her work.

Soon, they were in the flat and the door slammed behind them.

"Let's not waste time, in here!" Teddy said as he pushed Richard into the bedroom. They both fell onto the bed.

"No one can say you're not keen," said Teddy looking at Richard. "Oh, you are a very big boy aren't you!"

"I can't grumble," said Richard as they explored each other's' bodies.

Soon they were naked, and Teddy lay on top of Richard. "Okay shall I, or will you?" Richard smiled and licked his lips.

"Let's toss for it!"

Teddy reached for some change on the bedside table. "Heads or tails?"

"Tails!"

The coin flew into the air and they giggled as they tried to see the result.

"Okay," said Teddy "Come on, bottoms up!"

They made love ravenously and Richard marvelled at how he could take on such a monster appendage. Eventually they both climaxed and relaxed breathlessly on the rumpled white sheets.

"That was a turn up for the books," declared Teddy. "We must do it again sometime."

"My turn next time," laughed Richard slapping him on the bum. "Better get dressed, Gloria will be back soon."

They quickly got dressed, just as they heard Gloria's car draw up outside.

Gloria was in her office when Teddy and Richard appeared.

"I see you've got to know each other," Gloria said knowingly. "I suppose it takes all kinds to make a world, eh Teddy? Richard! Go and wash your face. It's very red, and I dare say that it's not only your face that's red! Now to business."

"Er, Richard brought these over from Wilfred," Teddy said swiftly.

"Get me the file on Weybridge, it's in the outer office," Gloria ordered.

Teddy did as he was told and disappeared into the other room. Gloria looked the papers over and liked what she saw. The new block that Wilfred had bought had good potential. It was a large house that could be turned into at least six flats. It was in a good area, and Wilfred had managed to acquire it from an old gentleman. The old man had wanted to end his life, where it began – in a tiny fishing village in Devon.

"We'll make a few grand on that!" she said rubbing her hands. "Is Wilfred pleased? He must be in a good mood."

"Yes, he's really excited. It's going to be a good day," said Richard, eager to please.

"I think it's already been a good day as far as you're concerned," said Gloria. "You'd better get back or he'll be wondering what's kept you."

"I'd better warn you," Richard said carefully, "Wilfred has heard that Teddy is back in the flat next door, and he's not pleased."

"Oh, shit!" This was news Gloria did not want to hear. "It must be that girl we have doing the cleaning. She's got a mouth like the River Thames."

"I would have thought that Teddy was just Abigail's cup of tea," Richard commented.

"He was! But he also drank from another cup! As you do sometimes!" Gloria declared bluntly. "Thank you Richard. I'll see you back home tonight, and do comb your hair. You look as if you've been dragged a hedge backwards, and take that silly grin off your face!"

***

Chapter Six

Emma was suddenly becoming more attuned to what was going on around her. She gradually realised that her brother, Teddy, had used her in an unforgiveable way. Her devotion for him was receding as time went on. She was a maturing young woman and now showed an interest in life and people around her which delighted both Aunt Clara and Alice. Sam had helped her acknowledge her role in the world and the fact that her talent for art was suddenly coming to the fore. She was able to do something worthwhile, and possibly earn her own living. Her affection for Sam was growing and she began to realise her capacity for earning real money. She was pleased that she didn't have to rely on people like Aunt Clara, however caring she may be, and her brother Teddy who was not! She had never had financial support from Teddy, and she never would. Only now, she would not even welcome it, even if it was suggested.

Frazer was another who had opened a door, and released her from being a nervous and fragile creature to a more responsive young lady. Frazer had been delighted with their dinner together. Emma's sudden interest in the world was tangible and it gave him much pleasure. It also gave him valuable information for his novel. He had paid Teddy the forty pounds for his introduction to Emma, and then had torn into him about his disgusting treatment of her.

"You ought to be ashamed, but I know you're not," screamed Frazer. "Degradation means nothing to you. I fear for your soul, your very being and if anyone deserved punishment, it should be you."

"Alright," replied Teddy. "You've got everything off your chest. You got your money's worth. I'm busy and it's time you pissed off!"

"Your time will come," said Frazer and, without a backward glance, he stormed off.

***

Julian Butler couldn't believe the enthusiasm that Emma's butterfly designs were mustering. The committee were impressed and delighted about the contract, and were equally enthusiastic about the company landing a new product. Sam was viewed in a new and more appreciative light and promotion was becoming obvious.

***
*

Gloria kept a close eye on Teddy, and marked his card as new clients came and went viewing new properties. She realised that she had tasted the wine herself, and probably would again, but Teddy toasting his wares to her clients was another matter. That was a worrying one. To get a sale within shouting distance and then to lose it because of Teddy, was something that couldn't happen. It was something that shouldn't happen, and could not be tolerated in any way.

Wilfred had calmed down a little over Teddy residing next to the office.

His disapproval however, had not evaporated.

One day, Angela Witherspoon arrived. Her splendid figure was dressed in the latest label and her blonde hair framed in what could be described as a nineteen thirties profile. She was not dissimilar to Jean Harlow and was most distinctive. She was forty-five and a very attractive woman.

Gloria was impressed and she didn't impress easily.

"Mrs. Witherspoon?" Gloria asked politely.

"I am she," Angela Witherspoon inclined her head regally. "I liked the literature that you sent me, and that large house in Woodland Way has caught my attention. Have you a day when I can inspect the property? It is unfurnished I presume?"

"Yes, it's only just come on the market," replied Gloria.

"Splendid!" Angela was pleased.

Gloria opened her diary "When are you and your husband free?"

"Oh! He departed to the other world several years ago, so he won't want a viewing," Angela giggled. "I'm a merry widow!"

"How about tomorrow afternoon at three?" Gloria suggested.

"That's suitable and convenient," Angela replied, pleased. "I presume that you have a young, reliable salesman to show me around – not an old fossil ready for the cemetery!"

"I have a young, charming gentleman who certainly knows the game,"

Gloria smiled.

"Until tomorrow then," Angela was delighted.

"I'll arrange it," Gloria made a note in the diary.

"Capital!" Angela exclaimed. "Good day Mrs. Trent."

"The name is Gloria."

"Thank you, Gloria," Angela smiled happily. "Till tomorrow at three."

With that, Angela Witherspoon sailed out of the office and was gone.

Gloria started thinking. This was one cookie that Teddy must not mess up!

Perhaps she'd get another man to show her around. But – Michael, her other employee, wouldn't attract a fly in a famine. No, it had to be Teddy.

***

Aunt Clara arrived and inspected the house. Yes, Emma had done the house proud. The carpets were hoovered, the brass was polished and the floors had been scrubbed. Aunt Clara wondered whether Emma had done it all herself, or perhaps Alice had given her a hand. Anyway, all was clean and tidy, and Clara was pleased.

Julian Butler's first cheque for five hundred pounds was safely in the bank in Emma's new account. It would stay there. Clara had Emma's cheque book and she had the authority to sign any cheque, which wasn't necessary at the moment. She felt she had been a little casual with young Sam. He had come in most handy, and proved to be an asset. She would remedy this. The doorbell rang and it was Alice.

"Good, I was wanting to talk to you, Alice," Aunt Clara ushered Alice in.

"I am impressed with the house being so clean and tidy. Emma has done a good job."

"Yes, she has. Clara, I need to talk to you about Emma."

"She's not ill or anything?" Clara was suddenly alarmed. "Let's have it!"

"Well," Alice began, "a quite well-known young man has been here and taken Emma out to dinner."

"Why wasn't I told?" Clara exclaimed in alarm. "The very idea! A girl like Emma, commandeered without my knowledge! Really, Alice, this is most disturbing."

Alice coughed nervously. She couldn't understand why Aunt Clara always upset her. She was only a woman after all.

"It was Frazer Lloyd, the actor," she murmured.

"You mean that blond man on the television who thinks he can act? The very idea!" Clara frowned. "What is he up to? That's what I want to know! You know what actors are like. All talk and no knickers! Alice, I really don't know what's come over you."

Alice opened and shut her mouth. She was beginning to get ruffled.

"You haven't even met Frazer," she offered gingerly.

"Oh! Now it's Frazer, not Mr. Lloyd," Clara exclaimed angrily.

Alice took the bull by the horns. "I met him and he is a very nice young man, even if he is an actor!"

"Well, he wouldn't pull the wool over my eyes, that's for sure!" Clara snapped. "What is he after? He didn't call for services, I hope!"

"On the contrary, Clara," Alice replied quickly. "He seemed very interested in Emma. I was here all the time when he called for her."

"You weren't present when he took her out to goodness knows where! I expect that's another story," Clara declared cynically.

"Oh, he took her to 'Le Plaisir' – a very fashionable restaurant for stage people," Alice said.

Clara drew herself up to her full height. "I know that sort of restaurant! They don't go there for food. They go to gape at each other. Like birds in a cage."

Alice took a deep breath. "May I continue?" she replied bravely. "The evening went well. Emma described the food. Some of the dishes I haven't even heard of, and she had a lovely time."

"I'd better have a little chat with Emma, and be brought up to date!" Clara declared angrily. "I must say, Alice, you seem to get easily carried away!"

"It depends who with!" Alice was delighted she'd got one over Clara.

***

On the dot of three, the next day, Angela Witherspoon arrived.

"Gloria. I have an appointment I believe, and I've brought a friend along with me for a second opinion. Rowena Courtney and she knows a thing or two about property."

"How do you do," said Gloria as she eyed Miss Rowena Courtney, a large lady of about sixty with glasses. Rowena's hair was pulled up into a chignon and she was formally dressed in black. Angela was dressed in designer jeans and a loose flowered blouse.

"Do sit down," Gloria invited. "Teddy will be with you shortly. Can I get you coffee?"

"No, thank you." Both ladies shook their heads.

They sat and waited. Teddy was ten minutes late. He arrived breathless, having run up the stairs. He was wearing a pale blue suit and an open white shirt. The trousers were rather tight around the crotch, and his striped blue tie was hanging tantalisingly from a pocket.

"I'm sorry I'm late, er ladies." He bowed.

"I should think so too," said Angela.

"This is, Teddy, ladies. Mrs. Witherspoon and Miss Courtney." They shook hands and the formalities were over.

"My apologies," Teddy declared. "I'll make it up to you."

"I'll make sure that you do," Angela said. "Time is money the good Lord says, Teddy."

"How true," added Gloria.

"Shall we proceed?" Angela asked. "My car is outside. Do you drive?"

"Of course!" Teddy loved to drive.

"Here are the keys," Angela dropped them into his hands. "I'm glad you can do something right. Come."

Angela swept out of the room like a galleon in full sail with Rowena trundling along behind her. Teddy obediently followed with a backward glance at Gloria.

He would have his hands full with those two, thought Gloria, with a smile.

***

Emma was nervous and flustered. Aunt Clara asked so many questions.

"This Frazer Lloyd," Aunt Clara looked severely at Emma. "What are his intentions regarding taking you out to dinner?"

"I really don't know," Emma said.

"Where did he come from, Alice?" Aunt Clara was determined to have all the information.

"I think Teddy knew him," Alice offered.

"That doesn't surprise me," Aunt Clara turned to Emma. "Did you misbehave?"

"Oh, no!" Emma exclaimed. "There was nothing like that."

"Like what?" asked Clara sharply.

Emma looked alarmed. "I don't know what you are on about Aunt Clara."

Alice quickly intervened. "Clara, you're upsetting the poor girl."

"Facts must be uncovered in a situation such as this," snapped Aunt Clara.

"Really, Alice!"

Gradually, Emma recounted the details of her evening out, the restaurant, the food and the clientele.

"I've heard about the restaurant, Emma," Aunt Clara stated. "I'm not a hermit! How did the evening end?"

"Frazer brought me home," Emma smiled at the memory. "He had such a lovely car, Aunt Clara. You have no idea."

"Unfortunately I do have an idea," declared Aunt Clara, "and you have nothing else to say?"

"Not really," Emma shook her head. "He made a lot of notes during dinner."

"Ah ha!" Aunt Clara exclaimed. "Notes! Now we are getting somewhere. What kind of notes?"

"I don't know," Emma shrugged. "Just notes."

"I'm sorry I had to ask so many questions." Aunt Clara seemed satisfied.

"Next time, ask my permission. Is that clear?"

"Whatever you say, Aunt Clara," Emma agreed.

"I should think so!" Aunt Clara replied. "Now go and watch television in the front room,"

"Alice!" Aunt Clara said as Emma left the room. "I want to meet this young man if he appears again. Things are not what they seem."

Aunt Clara checked the geraniums in the window box.

"Alice! These haven't been watered since Good Friday!" she stated. "See to it."

***

Teddy drove the two ladies to Woodland Way. Angela eagerly pushed Rowena along the hallway towards the stairs.

"We'll look at the upstairs first," she declared. "Four bedrooms, I think. What was your name again young man?

"Teddy!"

"Teddy what? You must have a surname," Angela looked him up and down.

"Jones, Teddy Jones."

"A popular name, I gather. Been with Gloria Trent long?"

"A few months."

"Then you've had to learn this game quite quickly," Angela commented. "I like a quick man."

"Mrs. Witherspoon," began Teddy.

"Call me Rowena, have you got the measurements of each room?"

"I've got all the details on my iPad."

"Yes, Gloria will have…" started Teddy, until he was cut off with a raised hand.

They looked at all the rooms and Angela particularly liked the master bedroom which sported a large, built-in circular bed.

"Hmm. I like that," Angela said with a knowing smile.

"It turns round, I'm told," said Teddy.

"What a novelty!" Angela exclaimed. "Now, we'll go downstairs."

Rowena and Teddy followed in Angela's wake as she swept downstairs.

Teddy had been taken aback, he hadn't expected this. He was beginning to enjoy the experience. They went through the small study, the enormous lounge, the capacious dining room, the well-fitted kitchen and the utility room.

The conservatory was a delight.

Angela clapped her hands. "I like it, Rowena! What do you say?"

"I agree," Rowena nodded in agreement.

"Of course you do," Angela replied. "It's beautifully laid out."

Teddy smiled to himself, so would Angela be with any luck!

"Rowena," Angela ordered. "Go and have a look around the garden and make notes. Lots of notes! List the flowers!"

"Ok," Rowena said as she exited through the conservatory into the garden.

Angela turned to Teddy. "Now, big boy, upstairs, and we'll see what you are made of."

In no time at all, they were in the master bedroom with the large circular bed. Angela grabbed Teddy's trousers and almost ripped them off.

He dealt with his shirt while she fumbled below. His penis stood like a ramrod, and he felt the warmth of her mouth as she tried to swallow the long, thick shaft.

Gradually, she released her lollipop and worked slowly up his firm six pack, to his hard nipples.

"Now!" she said triumphantly. "Let's see what this bed can do, and you can show me what you're made of!" She dragged him onto the revolving bed and he entered her with ease.

"More, more, more," she screamed as the bed rotated and Teddy did his stuff. It was over quickly and they were both surprised at the intensity of their passion. They lay back watching the circling ceiling as Rowena entered the room.

"Well, that wasn't bad, Teddy," said Angela. "Now, Rowena, it's your turn!"

Rowena took off her glasses and undid her hair which fell seductively around her shoulders. Her dress fell effortlessly to the floor, and she lunged at Teddy. Teddy had the feeling that he was being used. This was new for him, but he didn't care and his glistening member rose again.

Rowena looked seductively into his eyes. "I like it slow!" she said sitting on him.

"Madam, you can have it any way you like," Teddy declared as he rammed his pride and joy into her. The size and length of his member surprised her and she gave out a delighted squeak at the intrusion.

"Oh, she's always a little timorous, Teddy, but she's desperate to be serviced all the same," Angela stated. Teddy's hands fondled Rowena's swaying boobs and ample nipples.

An hour later, after much excitement and several rotations of the bed and bodies, Teddy was exhausted and retired to the bathroom to recover while the ladies dressed. He got dressed and found that his legs were quite unsteady as he descended the stairs and drove the ladies back to the office in their car.

"I'll call Gloria in the morning," declared Angela as they arrived back at the office.

Teddy climbed out of the driving seat and Rowena came round to take over the wheel. With a well-aimed slap on Teddy's backside, Rowena slid into the driving seat.

"Bye," Angela called out as they sped off up the street.

Chapter Eight

Aunt Clara couldn't believe that Emma's talents could have earned such a massive sum of money. It was bordering on the ridiculous. She had to think where and how she could invest the amount that a mere butterfly design had earned. The other factor was that Emma was beginning to cope more with her maturing life. It was as if someone had found a key and it was slowly opening a door to a new world.

Alice had noticed the change as well and mentioned it to Joe, her husband.

"You know the vicar at St. Thomas's, Joe?" she asked.

"Yes," said Joe half-heartedly.

"The one that married us," Alice continued. "Well, do you know, he has a boyfriend?"

Joe grinned at her. "Well, that's put paid to the dream I had of you running off with the vicar!"

Alice beamed at her husband.

"It means…"

"I know what it means, you silly woman," Joe chuckled. "The vicar's gay.

So what! Let the man be happy. At least, he's got someone to collect the prayer books, and that saves you the bother."

Alice was proud of her Joe. He rarely saw any harm in anyone.

"What else do you want to tell me, Alice?" Joe knew her well. "You're dying to tell me something."

Alice told Joe all about Emma's contract with Julian Butler and Greystone to publish her design and the sizeable income that came with it.

"Good for Emma," exclaimed Joe. "Now, you'll find that she'll start realising that there is something else in life. I presume Clara will be dealing with it on Emma's behalf; you couldn't do better than that. As long as Teddy doesn't get his hands on it. That boy will come to no good I'm afraid."

"I took Emma to church today, and she found it fascinating," stated Alice.

The vicar, the choir, the collection, and the churchgoers, it was like a peep into wonderland and she loved it!"

"This is all good news, Alice," Joe was proud that Alice was helping Emma so much. "Pass the mustard there's a good girl. Beef without mustard is like strawberries without cream!"

"I think we are going to see a different Emma from now on," Alice said.

"Until the next time Teddy Jones gets hold of her!" Joe remarked cynically.

"No, Joe!" Alice exclaimed. "That's where you are wrong."

"I certainly hope so!" Joe murmured as he tucked into his Yorkshire pudding.

***

Teddy wandered into town after a busy day showing people round houses. He was as randy as a peacock on heat. There was a new club which had just opened and he felt it was worth a visit. It was situated down an alleyway in a basement underneath Boots the Chemist.

A rather fey young man was at the desk.

"Membership card!"

"I didn't know it was a members club!" Teddy answered.

"You have to apply," the young man replied firmly. "Membership forms are over there on the right."

Teddy was a little bit taken aback, but he sat down and filled the form in. It comprised mainly of personal details, name, address, references, date of birth and occupation. He duly filled it all in and handed it back to the chap on the desk.

"My name's Rupert!" The young man smiled.

"Well, fancy that!" Teddy snapped, not at all impressed with this man's interrogation.

Rupert read the form, made notes, and managed a half smile.

"Sixty pounds, please," he held out his hand.

"That's a bit steep," Teddy objected.

"So are the Cliffs of Dover," Rupert grinned cheekily. "We do take cards."

Teddy duly produced his American Express Card and was issued with a membership card.

"Straight through those doors and the bar is on the right," Rupert stated.

"Perhaps I don't drink," replied Teddy.

"Pigs might fly!" replied Rupert impudently.

Teddy went into the large lounge on the right of the door. It was fairly crowded with a mixture of both sexes. He found a seat next to a tall blonde with a little too much lipstick and eye shadow, but Teddy could cope with that.

"Been here before?" he asked.

"Yes," the blonde said as she sipped her large gin and tonic. "Do you live far away?" she asked.

"Far enough," replied Teddy. He noted the large string of pearls and the several large rings on her fingers. She seemed to have a few bob.

"Cabaret's at eight!" she declared.

"I don't think I'll be here that long," said Teddy. "Just fancied a quick drink."

"There are two bars in here and there's a smaller one over there. I'll take you in if you like." She smiled showing perfect, white teeth, and eased herself sexily off her bar stool. The small bar was deserted and they stood in the dimly lit room. The black barman had disappeared and they were alone.

Teddy thought he would make a play and put his hand on the girl's left tit.

Suddenly, she turned towards him, looking deeply into his eyes. "Actually, I am a man!"

"Oh!" said Teddy, a little taken aback. "I suppose that's all right. I swing both ways."

"Not with me you don't!" declared the blonde.

"Well, you shouldn't display the goods if they are not for sale," Teddy admonished.

The blonde lifted her wig for an instant and then reset it.

"Look, chum, you're not getting a fuck out of me. So close the book!"

"What's wrong with me?" asked Teddy.

"I just don't find you attractive," the blonde shrugged.

Teddy pursed his lips, what on earth was this guy's game?

***

Gloria arrived home late and tired. She helped herself to a drink and sank into a chair.

"I've had a hard day, Wilfred," she said.

"Pity." Wilfred's tone was hard. "You'll have an even harder day when I've finished with you!"

He showed her Abigail's letter.

"Now, do you understand?" he snapped. "I want this bastard out!"

"Abigail does get carried away," she said, quickly lighting a cigarette. "I understand that there was a little episode, but it soon blew over."

"Not according to Abigail," Wilfred muttered.

"Wilfred!' Gloria thought quickly. "You know that Abigail is a bit of a drama queen. I'm sure that she had her way with Teddy then got uptight when he had it off with the gardener."

"Is that so?" Wilfred glared angrily at her. "And what about you, Gloria? Do you taste his wine as well? Is that the state of play? I need to know, Gloria. I am your husband."

"I am well aware you are my husband," Gloria glared furiously at him. "I can't cope with your jealousy. I do a good job. I run the business really well. Profits are good and the office is run efficiently. I want to keep Teddy and that's that!"

Gloria stormed out of the room and slammed the door behind her.

The French doors to the garden opened slowly and Richard entered.

"Did you hear that?" Wilfred asked.

"Every word," Richard nodded.

"Well, let's get this straight," Wilfred declared. "We have to get rid of this stud. You'll have to help me, Richard.

"I am always here for you Wilfred," Richard smiled reassuringly. "You know that!"

Richard took hold of Wilfred's hand and gave him a peck on the cheek.

***

The barman returned and Teddy ordered another drink. He didn't offer one to the blonde.

"Don't I get one? You did enjoy a little fumble you know. My name is George, but you can call me Georgina."

He called the barman over and indicated Georgina. "Whatever he wants."

"Large gin and tonic coming up!" stated the barman.

Teddy threw a twenty pound note on the bar and told the barman to keep the change.

"No change out of a twenty mate," said the barman with a wry smile.

"I take it you're looking for a quick shag," said Georgina.

"How observant you are!" said Teddy raising an eyebrow.

"Well, I have an orchard full of cherries."

Teddy didn't know what he or she was on about.

"I have a small retinue of ladies who, shall we say, need a little special attention and like to be serviced regularly. Does that appeal to you?"

"Why are you in drag?" Teddy asked. "Dressed up like a tart!"

"In drag I may be, but the tart bit is not acceptable. Now if you like fucking the ladies, we could be in business."

"I don't get what you're after?" Teddy declared.

"Apart from my own desires, I run a club for over-sexed females, and I am always looking for a new stud. I will pay you depending on how good you are in the sack."

"How much?" asked Teddy his mind running wild with possibilities.

"A hundred quid a booking. Some of my ladies are loaded. You look well upholstered and can come up with the strong equipment required. Most of them live locally. Could we have a deal?" asked Georgina offering her hand. "I have a large flat off the High Street, so an address is no problem," she said.

Just then a tall muscular man came by with much to recommend him.

"Georgina! Got a spare afternoon?"

Georgina beamed. "For you, Roger, it's open hours forever."

"I'll ring you," he said as he headed into the main bar.

"I'm breathless for the call," called Georgina. She turned back to Teddy.

"Do we have a deal?"

"Yes, we have a deal. When do I start?"

"Next week. That is, if you are free."

"Can be!"

"Good, let's get down to business. I need a few particulars."

Georgina opened her bag and took out a pad. She took a photograph of Teddy on her phone and five minutes later all was agreed.

"My card," said Georgina giving him a glossy, red and gold embossed card.

Teddy looked at the card. "It's the same address as this club."

"Of course," said Georgina. "I own the fucking place."

***

Gloria was ill at ease the next morning. Upsetting Wilfred was one thing, but she did go out of her way to keep him happy and content. She knew he had it in for Teddy, and sooner or later Teddy would have to go.

Teddy looked extremely handsome that morning. Gloria noted a little confidence in his smile.

"I'll have to finish early next week, about five. I've got a new part time job," he announced.

"Where, for God's sake?" Gloria asked.

"A new club on the other side of town."

"What are you going to be doing?" Gloria was intrigued.

"That would be telling!" said Teddy with a twinkling smile.

"I'll get it out of you, sooner or later, just you wait and see," Gloria said. "Now, I have a nice couple for you today. Mr and Mrs Finch."

"Young?" asked Teddy.

"Past their sell by date," said Gloria with relish as his face fell. "No hanky panky, do you hear?"

"I don't go in for old roosters."

"From what I hear, you'll go for anything breathing!" said Gloria handing him his property brief.

"Don't listen to rumours, Gloria dear, it can lead you in dark waters."

The telephone rang and Gloria answered it, Teddy went into the outer office.

"Another prospective client, Teddy," she called out.

"That's encouraging," he replied from the other room.

Gloria had a sudden thought of how to humour Wilfred. She would put an ad in the local paper for a new salesman. That would do it! It might even pay dividends one way or another.

***

Alice couldn't get over how Emma had taken to the church. Emma insisted that she helped Alice collect and place new flowers and noted how Alice arranged the flowers to the greatest effect. Aubrey, the vicar, noticed all this with enthusiasm. He liked Emma, even though he thought she was a little strange.

"I would like to welcome you to Saint Thomas's. I am the vicar of this parish, and Alice is one of my most ardent followers," said Aubrey with a smile.

Emma was pleased. All this was new to her, especially as religion had never played a part in her life before.

"The church is like an old friend, Emma. We are always here when you need help or advice, or just to worship."

The last bit flummoxed Emma a little, and a frown flittered across her face.

"Everything will make sense to you in time, Emma. We must remember that Rome wasn't built in a day!"

"I don't know anything about Rome!" said Emma.

"I don't know much about Rome either, but that doesn't matter. It matters that you have discovered us. I mean the church!"

"Who pays the rent?" asked Emma.

"Oh! There are many contributors to the church. Alice, I do admire your guidance with dear Emma. It's what the church is all about."

"I am so pleased, dear Vicar. I am so sorry I am not able to spend as much time as I used to, to help you in your work."

"Oh, come now Alice. You are the most devoted of my flock. I really don't know what I would do without you."

Emma found the collection box.

"Is this for the rent, Mr. Vicar?" she asked.

"Sort of," he replied.

"Then I've got some money in my pocket I'd like to put in." Emma placed the coins carefully in the box.

"Thank you, my child," said the vicar, and Emma beamed.

***

Teddy was looking forward to the new job. A hundred quid for fucking a willing lady! This was nectar from the Gods!

George, or Georgina, had given him three clients, and the address of the discreet flat she had off the High Street. His first date was in the evening and the girl's name was Sadie. He rang the doorbell, and she let him in. She was tall with long brown hair, with a long angular face and enormous eyes.

"You're Teddy."

"That's right."

145

"I'm Sadie. I hope you are experienced. I am madly sexual, but lovely with it."

"I'm glad to hear it!"

She led him into a large room which sported a big king-sized bed, a drinks trolley and two chairs.

"What's your tipple?"

"Whisky!"

"That's a promising start," said Sadie as she poured two large measures into two of the cut glass tumblers.

"I've made them doubles," she said as Teddy took off his jacket.

"Great, thank you. How long is our session?" he asked.

"As long as you can keep it up, darling!"

"I've never had a complaint!"

"I'm glad to hear it," she said confidently.

Teddy was curious. He sat in the chair and lounged back with his drink.

"What do you do for a living – if it's not a rude question?" Teddy asked.

"I don't do anything, darling. Daddy's rich as hell and I get bored."

He chucked the whisky down his throat with one go and placed the glass back on the trolley. She started to undress him slowly. He slipped off his shoes while she undid his shirt, she ran her lips over his hard body. His trousers were off in a flash, and she quickly shed her dress and slip. She didn't wear a bra, and only wore a tiny G-string.

"I like to do the undressing," she said as she knelt before him and slowly pulled down his briefs. His large erection lurched out of the material, nearly knocking her in the face.

"Bloody hell! Not bad! Not bad at all!" she said with relish.

"I'm glad you are pleased," said Teddy with satisfaction.

"Ooooooh! Looks juicy," she exclaimed as she studied his ten inch wonder.

Suddenly, she hauled his dick into her mouth, and sucked him as if he was an orange. A couple of minutes of this and Teddy was scared he was going to finish early. However, his body obeyed, and she continued licking and teasing.

"Right," she commanded suddenly. "On the bed and let's have all ten inches of it!"

He thrust his equipment into her as if there was no tomorrow and her squeals of delight were pleasing.

"More, more, shove it right up!" she commanded.

"Madam, I am your slave," he replied thrusting deep inside her.

"Too right you are," replied Sadie.

They were in the throes of passion for at least four minutes when he suddenly came with much force.

"Waw," he said. "How was that?"

"The best I've had this month," she replied. "You're nice and thick which is a bonus. I'm very pleased." She got up and walked to the en-suite bathroom. Her tits seemed to be in the act and her nipples almost danced to her rhythm.

"Have you had your money's worth, Sadie?" asked Teddy.

"It'll do for now. I like your body, you have a nice ass, and your cock is tremendous."

For a moment he suspected that she wanted a replay, but she threw him his briefs.

"Here, get dressed. I'll pour us another drink. I've got more games I can introduce you to next time," she murmured. "You collect your cheque at the club."

He paused. She was so bloody clinical. Perhaps her father owned a string of laboratories. They dressed and she covered her voluptuous body.

With a slightly shaking hand, he finished his whisky quickly.

"You haven't met my sister, Rita!"

"No, I haven't met anyone. You are my first."

"Oh, you'll need all your gunpowder for Rita. You won't be able to walk when she's finished with you."

"Thanks for the warning," said Teddy limply. "Well, I must go. Sadie it has been a pleasure."

"Likewise," she said licking her lips.

She took him to the door, and he was gone.

***

Daisy turned up again at the office. She looked 'tatty' and she was not in a good mood.

"Can I help you?" enquired Gloria. Gloria was in no mood for this woman after her visit last time.

"I'm here to see Teddy Jones!"

Gloria told her in no uncertain terms that Teddy was not there.

"What if I don't believe you!" slurred Daisy.

"Then you go out of that door," Gloria said forcefully as she gave her a shove. "Out!"

Daisy gave Gloria a nasty look and raised her hand as if to hit her.

"Ok I'll go, but I'll be back."

Gloria smiled a dangerous smile.

"Somehow I don't think that's a good idea," said Gloria as she propelled Daisy through the doorway, and slammed the door. This was something she could do without!

***

Emma was on her own when she received a telephone call. It was Herbert and he asked if he could have an appointment! Emma hesitated. What if he wanted a session? Clara would be there soon, and what about Alice?

She liked Herbert. He was a poor lonely soul who lived in the world of literature. He didn't seem to have any friends, and his family obviously had no time for him.

"It is Emma, isn't it?"

"Of course, when do you want to come?"

"Can I come tomorrow at three?"

"Yes. Aunt Clara may be here, but we can always go to my room to talk. Will that be alright?"

"That would be wonderful. I have to talk to someone about my working career. I need to ask a friendly person if I am doing the right thing or not."

"Do come," Emma seemed to understand. "You remember where to come?"

"Oh yes, I remember. You're a very nice girl, Emma. I remember everything we talked about last time. See you tomorrow."

***

Georgina had arranged that Teddy would meet Rita, at the same flat a couple of days later. He was pleased with the way that the evening with Sadie, her sister, had gone, and he was sure she had received her money's worth. She had been a tornado and she had said that Rita would be explosive! Never was a truer word spoken!

He turned up at the appointed time and let himself in with the key Georgina had given him. There on the large bed was Rita! She was sixty if she was a day, and scored a big zero in the looks department.

"So, you're the wonder boy!"

"I don't follow?"

"You're the male whore!"

"I beg your…" started Teddy, taken aback.

"You're the new stud who is supposed to provide me with sex!"

"I don't think so."

She stared angrily at him. "I think so."

"You're old and ugly and no way am I going to service you!" Teddy stated flatly.

"Is that so?" snarled Rita.

"That is so! You should have retired years ago, you tired old fruit."

"I don't like your tone," barked Rita.

"Pity!" Teddy declared. "I'm going. I'm not going to have sex with an old crone like you."

"You listen to me, boy," snarled Rita. "I have power and I have associates. If you don't alter your tone I'll get one of them to fix you, good and proper."

"Threats don't work with me. You can go and fuck yourself!" Teddy turned on his heels and stormed out.

"You'll be sorry," she screamed, but she screamed to an empty room. Teddy had gone!

***

150

***

Teddy decided not to go to the club that night, so he hurried homeward. He needed a drink. As he turned the corner, he saw a man lurking in the shadows. He was a tall chap dressed in black and Teddy had seen him several times before. It was always late at night, lurking in the shadows. Teddy decided that it did not really concern him and, anyway, he had other things on his mind.

***

Herbert came to visit Emma. As before, he was not a minute early, and not a minute late. Emma kissed him and helped him off with his coat.

She was pleased that Clara had gone out shopping, and would be gone for some time.

"It is nice to see you, Herbert," she said hanging the coat up in the hall.

"Oh, Emma. I have been looking forward to seeing you again so much. I hope you are not 'in service' anymore." He didn't quite know how to phrase that last remark, and blushed profusely.

"Oh, no," said Emma matter-of-factly. "Aunt Clara looks after me now."

"She's not here?" he said shaking with nerves.

"No, she's not. It's just you and me. Are you still at the library?"

"Yes. That's really my home and all I care about. You see, Emma, I don't seem to be like other chaps of my age. I don't care for sex, I just like company. I know I'm not good looking, but I am a good person.

151

The family have no time for me. They have their own lives which really doesn't include me. My mother feeds me, and I have my own room.

Her life is full of meetings and committees and running about town.

So, I really am on my own. Do you understand what I am trying to say?"

Emma took his hand in hers.

"I think so, Herbert. I'm not considered very bright, but my life is suddenly changing and I am finding it easier to understand more.

People are beginning to include me in their conversations and not think of me as part of the furniture."

"Oh, I can sympathise, Emma."

She began to tell him all about Sam and her butterfly designs and intimated about the massive sums that she would be earning.

"It's all due to Sam. He's very young, and he came to me to lose his virginity," she declared.

"Oh!" Herbert looked embarrassed. "I should keep that to yourself, Emma, if I were you."

Emma smiled sweetly. "That's all water under the bridge now. I don't do that anymore. Sam and I are great friends."

Herbert smiled. "Your brother used you so cruelly, but things are beginning to come right now aren't they?"

They sat and chatted and Herbert told her of his dream of setting up his own bookshop.

"I have saved some money, Emma, and I know a small shop which is empty and in a good position. Do you think I should have a go?"

Emma didn't realise what having a go was, and Herbert explained as simply as he could.

"It's being my own boss. I know books like the back of my hand. The rent for the shop is cheap and manageable."

Emma clapped her hands, and thought the undertaking was quite exciting.

"I've saved over five thousand pounds so far."

"Does your mother know?" asked Emma.

"She wouldn't know if I swam the channel."

"Could I come and help you in the shop?" Emma asked excitedly. "I love books and I read all the time."

"Would you?" asked Herbert.

"I would love to. I'll have to ask Aunt Clara, and maybe Sam. I could give you some of my money. Isn't it wonderful!"

"I could make you my partner!" said Herbert enthusiastically.

"Oh, thank you Herbert. You'll have to meet Aunt Clara when you come again. Anyway, I will speak to her."

"I'd better go now. You don't mind me coming to talk to you?"

"Of course not!" said Emma. "It was lovely to see you."

"I'll be in touch soon, then."

Herbert left with a spring in his step.

***

Teddy returned to the office a little crestfallen. His experience with Rita had not been a happy one. Gloria tried to talk to him, but he didn't want to know.

"Did you notice that strange man in black as you came in?" she asked.

"No, not particularly," Teddy answered shortly.

Gloria looked out of the window. "Oh, he's gone now – strange fellow. He's been there before. He just stands watching. Now, Teddy, I've got some clients for you this afternoon."

"Good," Teddy was pleased. "I need something to do. I think Emma's come into some cash with her artwork."

"Oh, that's nice for her," Gloria said generously.

"It seems to be a big deal with her designs. You can't believe all you hear though. I can't get to grips with it because of Aunt Clara. You know what a cow she is."

"I'm sure you can handle her, Teddy. Emma seems to. By the way, are you still in the flat?"

"Yes, why?"

"Well, sooner or later, Wilfred's going to wander in. So you'd better be on the lookout for a new pad. Now – the clients this afternoon. The name is Holman. Looking for a flat. The wife seems to know you."

Teddy gathered the details and headed out of the door.

***

Chapter Nine

Georgina gave Teddy a sharp look, she really was not pleased. She looked at Teddy and her eyelashes waved as if in a storm. She had been looking for a male 'pro' for ages, and now that she had found one, he had disappointed her.

Georgina was to the point. "I think you have a cheek to turn up after your last appointment! Rita is furious and I have a row on my hands. You are the cause of it! Okay, you can handle the Sadie's of this world, but you have to take the rough with the smooth."

"Rita's an ugly old broad, and I do have some standards," said Teddy.

Georgina scratched her wigged head. Perhaps this Teddy Jones was not such a good idea after all. Rita was very powerful in the underworld and could cause him and Teddy much harm, and probably would.

Teddy grinned and thought it was a huge joke, or at least Rita was. He touched Georgina's face and told her that his lipstick wasn't straight.

Georgina was annoyed and repeated to Teddy that he was only on probation.

"I don't know how you get away with all this. The police could put a stop to it all," snapped Teddy.

"No, they won't," Georgina laughed. "I pay them far too much to keep their mouths shut, and you had better do the same if you know what's good for you."

Teddy realised that he had been foolish to return to Georgina, but his cash was low. The drugs he took cost a great deal of money and the nags didn't always run as promised.

Georgina knew it would not be easy to pacify Rita, but she would have to, somehow! She nodded to Teddy. "We'll give it another go."

***

Emma confided to Alice about Herbert's visit and proposal. She was really excited about the whole thing. However, she did wonder how she was going to impress Aunt Clara. Alice spoke some sense, but a few questions were still begging an answer.

"Did he come for, well... you know what?" Her face coloured up like a pomegranate, she was so embarrassed. Emma shook her head.

"No, Herbert's not like that, he only wants to talk," Emma snapped.

Alice thought she'd better leave it at that. She felt as if she was fishing in deep waters.

"Oh, Alice," Emma declared. "I do want to help Herbert start up on his own. He hasn't much else to look forward to."

Alice smiled. This young woman was really changing; Emma was going down a new road.

"You see," explained Emma. "He wants to set up his own small bookshop, and he knows how people follow authors and build up their libraries."

Alice didn't quite know how to put this, but she enquired if Emma was going to use some of her own money to help Herbert with his project.

"Yes," came the prompt reply.

Emma looked at Alice. She knew she had an ally, but then she thought about Aunt Clara. She wouldn't be over the moon at such a project.

"Listen," Alice declared. "If you are serious, Emma, it does sound like a wonderful idea. I will help you all I can to persuade Aunt Clara. You know I will."

"It's my money, Aunt Clara told me so," Emma said.

Alice smiled. "Yes, it is your money, my dear. You've earned it yourself. Aunt Clara is only looking after your interests. When she comes back from the shops, we'll try and persuade her to go along with your idea."

***

Teddy, eventually, after several large gins got another appointment out of Georgina, and she turned out to be a very young blonde. Her name was Rachel.

"I've never done anything like this before," she said as he let her into the flat. "Unfortunately my man isn't into sex."

"That's a shame," said Teddy. "He seems like a waste of time."

"Oh, he isn't," she said. "He's kind, gentle, pays all the bills, but he's gay. He likes men."

"It happens," said Teddy showing her into the bedroom.

"I want a baby!"

"Well," said Teddy unzipping his flies. "We'll see what we can do."

He gradually undressed her, taking his time, then when he had her naked, he laid her gently on the bed. He then quickly slipped off his shirt and trousers. His penis was already something to behold and strained against the soft material of his pants. Rachel was mesmerised.

"You are rather large, if you don't mind me saying so!"

"You pay by the inch," Teddy said with a laugh. "Let's see what we can do, shall we? No condoms eh? You do want a baby! Will your feller mind?"

"No, he's all for it!"

"How did you hear about me?"

"My feller, Sebastian, works at the club sometimes, and Georgina who knows us well, suggested a one-off for me."

Teddy laid her back on the crisp white sheets. He kissed her breasts, her navel, her inner thighs, and she sighed with pleasure.

"Oh, that's good, really good. Do take your time, I don't mind paying extra."

Teddy's tongue went into action and he licked her tender skin with fervour.

Gradually he slipped his throbbing tool into her.

"Okay?" he whispered.

"Yes, I am enjoying this," Rachel gasped. "You really are gentle."

He pressed further into her, enjoying her warmth and the gentle moans she made. Passion took over and soon they were thrashing around in ecstasy. He came suddenly and powerfully.

"Oh! Goodness!" squealed Rachel. "Crumbs, you're very experienced!"

"I am!" smiled Teddy as he withdrew.

"Why do you fuck girls like me who you really don't know?" Rachel asked.

"It suits me," said Teddy, relaxing back on the pillows. "I like shagging and if I can make a few pounds doing it, that's for me."

"Do you have a regular girl?"

"Not particularly."

Rachel sat up, "You are very well made. My Sebastian is, but I have a job turning him on. I wonder if we've made a baby!"

"Time will tell," said Teddy as he gave her a monster kiss. "I like you, Rachel."

"I like you too," she said.

"We must do this again," Teddy declared. "Here's my card, and don't go through Georgina."

Rachel dressed quickly and Teddy lay back on the bed enjoying the thrill of being admired.

"If you get pregnant, do let me know," he said. "If you don't, we'll try again!"

"I will," she said triumphantly. "You'd better put your clothes on, you'll catch cold."

Teddy dressed.

"Thank you once again," said Rachel as she hurried out of the door.

Teddy poured himself a large whisky as he thought about Rachel and her wanting a child.

***

Aunt Clara returned from her shopping and Emma and Alice were waiting nervously. Emma started to tell Aunt Clara about Herbert and his idea of a small bookshop.

"Who is this man, Herbert?" Aunt Clara demanded. "I certainly cannot place him, not even in the passing parade we seem to be witnessing."

Emma looked at Alice for support.

"We met him at the library," Alice said.

"I've not heard the library mentioned before!" Aunt Clara frowned at them both.

"It is usually an oasis for restless people, and I was asking Emma, Alice, if you don't mind."

Emma shifted nervously from one foot to the other. Clara was not impressed with the hesitation. Emma told her of the meeting and the discussion about authors.

Aunt Clara looked at them both suspiciously. Alice couldn't really tell which way this inquisition was going.

"This young man Herbert," Aunt Clara probed. "What is his background?"

Emma started fidgeting. "His mother has no time for him."

Aunt Clara snorted. "Really! That is hardly a recommendation. How long has he worked at the library?"

Alice tried to answer but was stopped with a cold look from Aunt Clara.

Emma finally said, "I don't know, Aunt Clara."

Clara paced the room. "It seems to me that you know very little about this Mr. Herbert Ramsey."

Alice had moved to another chair, and really did not know what to say.

Clara glared at her. "Don't fidget, Alice! Not good for the brain!"

Aunt Clara was enjoying this. She really liked being the headmistress, and she looked down on Emma as a guilty child. Emma was anxious to protect Herbert, yet she needed to get Aunt Clara on her side -not an easy thing to do, but then life was never easy.

Alice cleared her throat "What I think is…"

Aunt Clara stopped her immediately. "When I want your opinion, Alice, I will ask for it."

"As you wish," said Alice as she slumped back into her chair.

Clara tapped her fingers on the table as if deliberating which way to go. She took a deep breath "So, Emma, I understand you wish to work with this Mr Ramsey."

Emma nodded. "Herbert has his eyes on a little shop in Sutton Street."

Aunt Clara peered at Emma "Who is financing this little adventure?"

Emma retorted quickly "He has saved."

Aunt Clara looked at Alice and then back at Emma.

"So has the Salvation Army!" she stated. "He has saved to what extent?"

Emma was determined to stick to her guns. Alice wanted to help but the thought of disguising how Emma and Herbert met confused her.

Emma cleared her throat nervously. "I do want to work with Herbert, Aunt Clara."

Aunt Clara pursed her lips. "That is painfully obvious, Emma. The fact that you wish to contribute something to the universe is heartening. Many men, however, are looking for vulnerable young women, of which you are one, my dear. This Herbert Ramsey and his background need investigation!"

Emma started to twitch and shake. "Aunt Clara. I want this work and Herbert would make me his partner."

Clara's eyes narrowed, now they were getting somewhere.

"Indeed!"

"Yes, I want to do it. I want to do it! I must do it! Why don't you understand?" Emma's eyes welled up with tears.

Aunt Clara went to her and put her arm round her shoulders. "All right, Emma, much more of this and you'll stop the traffic! I don't mean to be demanding. I'm only trying to safeguard you and your future."

At that moment, the doorbell rang. "Alice, tell whoever it is that we are out!"

Alice gave her a look and did as she was told.

Emma took a deep breath and faced Aunt Clara. "I am grown up," she declared firmly. "I am not mentally unstable. I am not an idiot. Frazer Lloyd says I am not, Sam says I'm not and now Herbert says so too. Why, oh why, can't you understand?"

Emma started to cry.

"Alright," Aunt Clara sat down next to her on the settee. "I will meet Herbert what's his name and make sure everything is as it should be. Do you agree Emma?"

Emma nodded her head.

"Good, I am pleased! Now dry your eyes and we will have tea!"

Alice re-entered the room.

"Alice! Who was at the door?" asked Aunt Clara.

"Just that strange man again, all in black, asking for Teddy. I told him he wasn't living here anymore."

***

Teddy met Mr. and Mrs Murray at the new flats that Wilfred had acquired. He was an astute businessman around fifty year of age and his wife was a good sixty plus, and attractive with it.

Mrs. Murray greeted Teddy and remarked that they had met before, but Teddy couldn't remember. Mr Murray told Teddy that the children that he had had with his first wife had grown up. Now, he and his new wife were on their own, the couple had decided to downsize and a new flat seemed to be the perfect answer.

Gloria had stressed to Teddy that they needed a sale to keep Wilfred happy. Teddy thought that the flat was ideal and the price was just right for them.

They inspected the rooms with a critical eye, and they remarked that the road outside was fairly quiet. This was always a big plus with buyers.

Teddy was pleased and it looked as if the couple were going to buy. The wife reiterated that they had met before, but Teddy didn't remember, or thought it best not to remember. They shook hands and he ushered them off the premises. It was only then that he noticed the man in black in the shadows opposite. What the hell was he up to?

He said his goodbyes, and turned to look at the man again, but the man had disappeared.

One day, he might find out but, today, he had other things on his mind.

Teddy headed for the office.

Gloria was delighted and after a drink, he satisfied her every whim, which was saying something.

***

Aunt Clara had agreed with Alice to take Emma along to the library to meet Herbert. She had reservations about the whole affair, but Emma was so keen on embarking on this venture. She had a right to a future, but she would first get to know more about this literary fellow.

The library wasn't busy that day, which was just as well. Aunt Clara demanded a chair which Herbert furnished her with. Herbert acknowledged Alice, and noticed that Emma was somewhat smarter than usual. Clara had bought her a new cardigan and matching skirt which fitted Emma perfectly.

This was just as well as Clara got into a mood if she ever misjudged anyone's size.

"You are Herbert Ramsey, young man, an acquaintance of my niece?" Aunt Clara asked formally.

"Yes, Ma'am," Herbert was very nervous in the presence of this forbidding woman. He realised that he must please this dragon.

"Have you have been here long, young man?" Aunt Clara demanded.

"Oh, yes," Herbert answered eagerly. "I have worked here ever since the library moved here from the old warehouse."

"Your education?" Aunt Clara asked.

"Secondary school, Ma'am, where I excelled in history and literature," Herbert replied.

Aunt Clara pursed her lips. "That seems very satisfactory!"

"Herbert knows every author, Auntie," Emma interjected. "His memory is amazing."

"No doubt," said Aunt Clara, softening a little. "I gather you intend to go into business on your own. Is that correct?"

"Yes, Ma'am."

"You may address me as Clara. That is my name."

Alice had kept quiet which she thought was the sensible thing to do.

"Have you thought this venture through, Herbert?"

"Oh, yes, Clara. I've been plotting the whole blueprint for some time. I have built up many contacts in the trade, over the years, and I can often trace rare books that are very well received."

"What is your father's occupation?" said Clara.

"He was a professional man."

"Very proper and satisfactory. Well, to sum things up, Emma is very keen, and wishes to join you in this venture. She wishes to be in a working role, and to supply a little financial investment. I approve. Can I have the name of your bank?"

"Certainly," Herbert was delighted. "It's Barclays in Shaldon Place."

"Excellent! I know the bank well, and when we move forward, I will need a contract between Emma and your good self. Then you will be in business."

She turned to Alice who hovered behind her. "Has the cat got your tongue, Alice?"

Alice smiled wanly. "You were doing very well without any assistance from me, Aunt Clara, that I do declare!"

"Precisely!" She turned back to Herbert. "Well, Herbert Ramsey! What do you say?"

Emma couldn't contain her excitement any longer. "Oh! Herbert's so pleased. I know he is, and so am I, Aunt Clara. We will work hard and please everyone."

"That remains to be seen," said Aunt Clara. "I think I know what you are trying to say." Clara got up to go. "The chair could have been more comfortable, but no matter. I will check on your credentials, Herbert, and then we can draw up an agreement. What is the rent for this shop, pray?"

"Just two hundred pounds a week, plus extras of course."

"Two hundred! I hope it's worth it!" said Aunt Clara feigning alarm.

"Oh, it is!" cried Alice caught up in the drama. "I know the area and it is in a good position."

"You seem to know most areas well, Alice! I'm glad you've suddenly come to life. Now, Alice, Emma, I think it is time for tea and crumpets! Goodbye Mr. Ramsey."

"Thank you, Ma'am, I mean Miss Clara."

Clara turned to Alice. "The boy has manners, Alice, that is a good sign."

Emma couldn't contain her excitement and jumped up and down.

"Stop it, Emma!" Aunt Clara looked disapproving. "You will do yourself a mischief!"

"Auntie, I am not a child anymore. I'm grown up now!"

"That remains to be seen," declared Aunt Clara.

Aunt Clara, Alice and Emma swept out of the library with Emma waving madly to Herbert. He took a deep breath and slumped exhausted into his chair. What was he getting in to?

***

Chapter Ten

Gloria sensed that Wilfred was changing. He was more alert, asking her to explain the tiniest detail. He didn't entirely trust her, but then he didn't entirely trust anyone. He knew that she was no angel, but then, neither was Richard. Richard did some clerical work for Wilfred, so he knew how the business was going. The talk about Teddy Jones had quietened down after Gloria's outburst. Richard had enjoyed his tumble with Teddy and was fascinated by him. He wanted more, and this time he would be on top!

***

Young Sam was excited. Julian Butler had told him that the first television commercial featuring the butterfly design and starring Frazer Lloyd would start being shown in less than two weeks. He would have to tell Emma. He rang her and she answered the phone. She was thrilled with the news.

"Oh, Sam it's all so exciting, and I made it all happen with my designs."

Emma suddenly remembered that he had something to do with it too.

"Of course you helped, too."

"It will feature Frazer Lloyd, a handsome blonde guy," he said. "I think you know him."

"Yes," Emma declared. "Frazer took me out to dinner. It was all very proper. He chose the food. I remember it all so well. Just think that through my designs, Frazer will be earning some money."

"A lot of money, Emma, quite a lot!"

"You know, Sam," Emma said pensively. "I've never thought much about money. My mother left me some so that I wouldn't starve and since Teddy, my brother, left I've quite enjoyed cooking. Isn't that odd?"

Sam smiled. "Not really odd, most women excel at cooking and creating new recipes, you know."

"Well, I didn't know," Emma said happily, "but I am beginning to catch on."

Emma told Sam all about Herbert and the new bookshop and, as she had hoped, he was most enthusiastic about the venture.

"I must ring off now, Emma," said Sam. "My telephone bill is going to be huge! Just think, when the bookshop opens, I will be able to pop in and see you, won't I?"

"Yes, of course!" Emma was delighted. "I hadn't thought of that. Herbert is very nice but he is a different kind of man. I read that the whole world is made up of so many varieties."

"You make it sound like a recipe for cooking, Emma," Sam chuckled.

"Oh, dear, there is so much to learn," cried Emma. "Will they cut you off if you don't pay the bill?"

"Probably," Sam laughed, "so I'd better go and make some money. We'll speak again soon."

"Bye." Emma put the telephone down and started to think. Everything was happening so fast. How could she cope with the excitement? Alice would help her. She was so kind and reliable. Emma suddenly remembered

Alice telling her about her little hat shop, and the fact that she was actually making hats. What a world it was!

**

Teddy decided that Georgina and the club were not worth the hassle. The money was agreeable but he felt he could do better elsewhere. The episode with Rita had unnerved him. She had become a bitter enemy and, if all he had heard was true, she could be dangerous.

Teddy was at a loose end and thought he would look Fay up. She was at her usual till at the supermarket checkout. Her pretty face was as delectable as always and, as far as he could see, she was no more pregnant than Snow White.

She seemed pleased to see him, and, when she had rung up his shopping, she winked at him.

"Friday?" Teddy asked.

"Why not!" Fay replied.

"Usual place?"

"Eight o'clock."

"Done." Teddy was delighted that his sexual attractiveness was as good as ever. Possibly she hadn't had many takers. He shuddered when he thought that daughters sometimes became like their mothers. Perish the thought!

At the office, Gloria was receptive as always. He thought that that woman could take on the world and then ask for more. There was the question of a new abode. Wilfred would sooner or later get him out of the flat, so this was becoming urgent. It was a pity that Abigail had caught him with the gardener and kicked him out. That could have been perfect, but there it was. These things happen, at least they did to Teddy Jones!

He hadn't quite grasped the whole situation with Emma. If what he understood was true, Emma was going to be a very rich girl indeed. Who would have thought it, his backward little sister! He had to get into that picture and quickly.

He could remember the day that Sam had called him. Talk about a tender virgin – but just look what had come out of that merger. He had only wanted Emma to taste the fruits of a sexual union. Talk about fate taking a hand!

Emma was blossoming and was no longer a fragile bloom. She was now a talented and useful female. The only cloud was Aunt Clara! She had to go, and soon! Then, he could sell the house and buy his own pad.

Then again, fate took a hand and he bumped into Wendy, the gardener.

***

Frazer couldn't believe that Emma had been commissioned for the commercial and he, out of hundreds of actors, had been chosen for the job. The commercial for the new soap would be worldwide, and it looked like a long running campaign, so that the money would keep coming in. His career had been drooping for some time. He was now thirty-six.

His hairline was already receding a little and his days of juvenile stardom would soon be over. Quite apart from his television work, the book he'd started was beginning to take shape. Emma was the central character and he was building on her fragility, but he had already observed the change in her. This could give way to a very interesting feature, and for many millions of people, give hope of maturing normally as the years go by. He

170

wanted to see Emma again and a dinner must be arranged. He quickly dialled her number.

"Emma? It's Frazer. Can we meet and have dinner again quite soon?"

"Oh, Frazer, I would love that!" Emma exclaimed. "Could we go to the same restaurant with the handsome waiters in jackets?"

"Why not!" Frazer smiled.

His agent had told him that the commercial would start in about two weeks' time. Frazer thought it would be marvellous to go out with Emma to celebrate when it was shown on television. He told Emma the date, and the dinner was arranged.

What wasn't arranged was the permission for the date with a woman known as Aunt Clara!

***

Teddy had two of Gloria's clients to deal with. Ladies of older years, he had a feeling they were lesbians. Both of them had been good looking in their day, but their faces were beginning to show the ravages of time. Like most females, they just couldn't make up their minds, so another visit to the flats would, no doubt, have to be arranged. As he ushered them out of the building, he noticed someone standing in the shadows across the road. It was the man in black again. What was he up to?

Teddy just dismissed him from his mind.

***

Wendy was shopping and she suddenly bumped into Teddy.

"There's a coincidence," she said. "I was just thinking about you."

"Then it was meant to be," said Teddy. He took her to a nearby coffee shop. Out of her gardening clothes she was very attractive, and obviously attracted to Mr. Jones. She was still working for Abigail Appleby and, somehow in the conversation, the question of a pad for Teddy came up.

"I've got a flat not two minutes from here," Wendy winked provocatively.

"Come and have a look. I'm looking for a lodger."

"Sounds like a good idea." Teddy's spirits rose. "Shall we go?"

***

Friday night came and Fay was waiting outside the supermarket. Teddy arrived, and had an idea. Wilfred's new flats were not too far away and he had a key. The flats were partially furnished, and there was one bedroom that had a bed! He called a cab and soon they were on their way.

Fay was impressed with the flats. She obviously came from a working class background. Daisy, after all, was as common as muck!

In no time at all Fay was admiring his body. Her breasts seemed larger than he remembered, and he licked and teased them, while her whole being quivered with excitement. She ran her fingers over his bulging crotch, and quickly tore off his trousers. Suddenly he sat up.

"What's the matter?" Fay asked breathlessly.

"Nothing really," Teddy said. "I just wondered how old you really are!"

"Does it matter?" Fay asked coquettishly.

"Not really, but I have had a visit from your mother."

"So what?"

Teddy frowned. "She said you were under age and demanded a large amount of cash from me to keep her quiet!"

"I'm afraid I let it slip about you," Fay looked apologetic.

"Silly girl. Actually how old are you?"

"I will be sixteen in a couple of months."

He felt his loins pulsating with passion. "Tough!" he said as her rammed his goods up her vagina.

They both reached orgasm simultaneously.

"Waw! How's that for instant enjoyment?" he cried.

"Wonderful." Fay gasped for breath.

"You're not pregnant, are you?" Teddy suddenly asked.

"Oh, no," said Fay. "Certainly not! I mean, we have been careful."

"That's what it says on my references!"

Fay stroked his chest. "Shall we have another go?"

Teddy rose again and slipped his body into hers effortlessly. They thrashed about on the bed until they were both spent, and even Teddy could do no more. Eventually, they tidied up the room and left the building. They said goodbye, not noticing a dark figure watching in the distance.

***

Emma had ideas forming for more artistic endeavours. With Sam's help, her hobby had turned into a strong financial endeavour. She started comparing different designs and new products appearing on the market.

Her mind was maturing all the time. It was as if some miraculous tablet had stimulated her interests and the monies that had so far arrived, gave her an entirely new outlook on life.

Alice was most helpful and assisted her in formulating new ideas. She was like a teacher discovering a genius in her class.

Clara couldn't believe that her sister's child was rapidly transforming her world. Her husband, listened to all Clara related, but couldn't quite grasp what it was all about. His marriage to Clara had started as one of convenience, but had matured into a loving relationship with sex hardly on the menu. Clara felt that she had to invest Emma's monies so she started studying stocks and shares. High finance was something that she had stumbled on and her interest was becoming considerable.

Alice was also making progress. Her hats were becoming fashionable. Recommendations were increasing and ladies from out of town were taking an interest. Clara's black hat had been widely praised and noticed.

Herbert was working hard on the bookshop and Emma helped him all she could. The opening was scheduled and everything was on track.

The whole panorama of the scene was exciting and demanding.

Emma hoped that she would be able to cope and enjoy the parade.

***

Wendy's flat was welcoming, carefully furnished and a home to be treasured. Well-tended plants were everywhere and the pale green walls gave it a calming atmosphere. There was more to Wendy than just a gardener however; there was a much darker side. He kissed her passionately, and she pushed him away.

"Now Teddy, before you get a total hard on, there is something else you can do for me."

"Yes," said Teddy not quite understanding what was coming next.

Wendy went to a cupboard and brought out a large case.

"I am into spanking," she declared producing a flat cane. "Will you smack my bum for me? I hope that won't put you off!"

"Not at all," said Teddy caressing the cane as he would a woman. In a trice, Wendy was naked and lying on her front with her buttocks ready for the attack.

'This is a turn up for the books,' thought Teddy.

Wendy took the spanking with delight and the markings on her bottom would have amused a zebra. After about sixteen strokes, she called for a recess. Teddy was quite pleased as his equipment had softened. This was different and his body was not amused. With a couple of large whiskies inside him, he returned to his normal self, and he and the gardener were satisfied.

"Well, do you like the idea of a lodger, Wendy?" Teddy asked.

"Absolutely, and you could provide a service instead of rent!" Wendy declared.

"Sounds most agreeable." Teddy strode over to the window and looked out. He had the strangest feeling that he was being watched.

***

Wilfred was getting bored, suspicious, and jealous. Richard was not as attentive as before. He seemed much more preoccupied, and as Wilfred noted every detail of those around him, he was curious.

Could he be servicing his wife, Gloria? Had he been co-opted by Abigail? Had he been seduced by Teddy Jones, or perhaps he had taken up religion? He knew that Teddy was still resident in the vacant flat, but he didn't want a stand up row with Gloria on the subject. She was much too precious. Sales were going well, so he didn't have to worry on that subject. His mind was still active, and he was constantly on the lookout for more properties to add to his stable.

***

Frazer Lloyd was very pleased with the commercial. The production company was adamant that it would be screened worldwide. It could revive his career and do him a power of good. He was extremely attracted to Emma, for apart from the commercial, he found her most intriguing, a fragile young lady who was just a little late flowering.

It was an affectionate friendship, and her character in his book was lovingly portrayed. It showed a person who needed guidance to make her life worthwhile. It showed how her life had been dominated by an older parent and how she achieved an interesting and attractive life despite the odds.

The minute the commercial was premiered and was shown on television, it could be a milestone for them both. Out of a misguided introduction had emerged a strong and tender friendship, that both of them would treasure through the years.

***

Richard received a telephone call from Abigail. She had a job that he could help her with. She knew that Wilfred depended on him and it was Wilfred who had introduced Richard to this clever and wealthy woman.

Richard had no intention of neglecting Wilfred, but some extra money would be useful. Abigail needed some rents and mortgages attended to and Richard made arrangements to see her.

The day was tropical, the sun blazed in a clear blue sky. When he arrived, he was directed to the swimming pool where Abigail was sunbathing. She greeted him with enthusiasm and he was astonished to see that she was nude!

"Hi, Richard! Thank you for coming!" She didn't choose her words carefully.

"Get your knickers off and enjoy the sun, while I tell you the little errands you can run for me."

Richard did as he was told and whipped off his shirt, trousers, and his boxer underpants and lay down beside her.

"I see you use the gym. So do I," Abigail commented eyeing him up and down.

"You're quite a big boy, I must say."

Richard was getting a little embarrassed as his cock lurched into action and shot up like a ramrod!

"I'm sorry, Abigail," he muttered, "but I seem to have got a bit aroused."

Abigail smiled and adjusted her sunglasses to get a closer look.

"I like something to look at to pass the time," she declared. "Would you rub some cream on for me?" She

177

turned over onto her stomach. "I hate to get burnt in any way."

Richard gently massaged the cream onto Abigail's back and she indicated that her front needed doing too. She turned over and her breasts stood up rigidly. He rubbed the cream all over her body, and suddenly he exploded!

It covered her and she lapped it up gratefully.

"Time to cool off," she said as she headed for the pool. "Come on!"

They jumped into the pool and work seemed a long way off. They embraced in the cooling waters.

"You really are a most obliging young man, Richard," she purred.

This was going to be a very interesting afternoon.

**

It was a changing scene for Clara Sullivan. For once in her life she had something to do other that look after Cyril. He only needed her for the usual married lady duties – cooking, cleaning, laundering, and the occasional bedroom tryst which didn't happen very often. Despite her quick tempered, hard, ill-mannered exterior, Clara, underneath, was a good, warm woman. Now, suddenly, she had something interesting to do, and it was all about Emma. Her own daughter Maisie, now lived in Canada, and was married to a salesman. It had not been a union that Clara approved of, and this had dented the mother – daughter relationship.

Clara had adored her sister, Rose, and missed her greatly. Now, she had to do her best for Emma.

**

Herbert was excited. The little book shop was his, the rental was agreeable, and now he had to build up his stocks for his discerning readers. His affection for Emma was strong, and she would be the support he needed. She was someone he could talk to. He was a nervous creature, instituted by his uncaring family. Now he was beginning to establish his own identity, a character was emerging and he was beginning to open up. He didn't know what to make of Clara Sullivan, but, no doubt, he would soon know her better! Emma had been a lost soul, but now she was showing such a lot of interest as her own life was unfolding. He looked forward to teaching her the tricks of the book trade.

***

Richard knew that his many absences from Wilfred would be noticed.

He would explain to Wilfred what had happened, and hopefully Wilfred would understand. He was fond of Wilfred, and he was one of the few who understood and sympathised with his condition. He was the lucky one.

He had survived the car crash unscathed. Wilfred had not been so lucky and such a blow would have destroyed most men, but not Wilfred Trent.

The day after his meeting with Abigail, Richard was back at Wilfred's.

"I think you have been having a little on the side, my boy, not that I am grumbling," said Wilfred with a smile.

"I was offered a little extra work. It's only for three or four weeks. It won't make much difference to my time with you, Wilfred."

Wilfred was intrigued. Could it be that Richard had a lover? Richard did seem a little more animated that usual.

"How did this come about?"

Richard wanted to tread carefully, but he knew that if he didn't answer honestly, Wilfred would find out in the end.

"Abigail Appleby rang me."

Wilfred nearly did himself a mischief. "That cow! She's like a crocodile on heat!"

Richard had to chuckle and he put his hands on Wilfred's shoulders. There was nothing that this man did not know.

"Apart from her so called work, she would have your dick in her mouth for breakfast!" stated Wilfred.

"Well, she got my number from you!" retorted Richard.

"That was before I knew what she was like!" laughed Wilfred.

Richard hesitated. He had actually enjoyed his 'by the pool scene', and his lady employer definitely knew every trick in the book to make a session pleasurable.

"We were by the pool and she asked me to put sun cream on her shoulders," Richard reported. "It was a very hot day yesterday."

"I bet it wasn't the only cream she enjoyed, yesterday!" Wilfred chuckled. "That woman is full of little games."

"How do you know?" asked Richard, intrigued.

"I've been there too, you know," Wilfred laughed. "She fucks like a rattlesnake! It was some time ago of course, but I've got a long memory."

Richard coloured slightly. He felt as if he had been used. It could all be part of Abigail's game. Wilfred suddenly burst out laughing. Abigail had a hunger that would shatter most men! He already knew that!

"Anyway, Richard, my advice is, don't give away your services for nothing," Wilfred warned. "How long does she need you, or, should I say, want you?"

"A month!"

Wilfred laughed out loud. "She'll drain you in a month! Just you be careful and taste the honey while it lasts."

Richard put his arms around Wilfred's shoulder and kissed him on the head.

"I'll be careful, I promise."

Wilfred enjoyed his gesture of affection. He must tell Gloria when she came home, it would go well with supper.

***

Chapter Eleven

Gloria had had a busy day and needed some relaxation. Teddy had gone to the flat early to rest, so she thought a visit would be a good idea. She took the spare keys from the safe and let herself into the next door flat.

She silently looked into the bedroom. Teddy was having a nap, wearing nothing but his briefs. She quickly shed her clothes and climbed over him and started playing. He awoke immediately and soon they were at it like hammer and tongs until exhaustion took over.

"I've got to go now," Gloria sighed. "Wilfred will be expecting me."

"Lucky chap!" remarked Teddy.

"See you in the morning," Gloria said as she gathered up her things and left the room. He would have to tell her soon that he was moving into Wendy's flat.

***

Alice's hat shop was becoming a great success. Having a business, although quite small, was encouraging and she loved her work creating hats. Her millinery was becoming popular and there were always weddings, funerals and fashion shows. She found the vicar extremely interesting and he was leaving the next garden party for her to organise. Her devotion to him and the church was absolute. Her work with the parish continued as usual, and on several occasions she had taken Emma with her.

Emma had been particularly fascinated with several cushions that the vicar owned. They had intricate, clever designs that had a religious bent. Glenn, the vicar's boyfriend, was also grateful that things were working out so well with his sister. Stella was not only a good sales person, but she was a pretty woman as well, which was a bonus. Alice was delighted to have her in the shop and she enjoyed Stella's company.

***

Herbert knew that Clara would try to interfere with setting up the bookshop, but he rapidly saw that some of her suggestions were spot on and helpful.

Emma was as excited as a schoolgirl and noted every author's work that she could. Aunt Clara decreed that readers expected a little knowledge about their choice of literature, and that a little knowledge was never a dangerous thing. Publishers had been most helpful, and astonishingly, they were willing to extend their books on approval, and only demanded sales money for goods sold each month. Clara was adamant about a good name for the shop. Herbert suggested 'Herbert & Emma' and she liked it immediately. It wasn't long before Teddy noted the shop and paid a visit.

Emma wasn't there that day, but Clara was! She showed him the shop door in no time at all!

***

The day was dull and murky and Gloria was not in a good mood. Richard was still 'working with' Angela. It could-be termed as having a 'man about the house'. Wilfred had been crotchety, and she had two new clients to sort out. She also had to organise Teddy. It was almost eleven o'clock and where the hell was he? Eventually, Gloria decided to go round to the flat.

Teddy was taking this too far. He might be a gift in the sack, but she had a business to run. She put her coat on and told the secretary in the outer office that she'd be back soon.

The front door of the flat was ajar, which was puzzling. Teddy was probably pissed and had forgotten to close the door thought Gloria.

"Get up you bastard," she called as she entered the hallway. There was no response, so she barged into the bedroom. Teddy was in the bed.

"Hello?" came a cheerful voice from the hallway. "It's Miranda! Oh, hello Mrs. Trent. I've just come to do the cleaning."

"You can help me get this man out of bed," muttered Gloria crossly.

Gloria went to the bed and shook Teddy. His eyes were tightly closed. Gloria slapped his face, but there was still no movement. Gloria was suddenly alarmed.

"Miranda, come and help!" she shouted.

Miranda and Gloria shook Teddy again, but there was no response at all.

"Is he dead, Mrs. Trent?" Miranda whispered in horror. "He looks so white!"

Gloria shook Teddy once more. There was absolutely no sign of life.

"Oh! My God!" Gloria cried. "He is dead!"

***

Shaking with shock, Gloria and Miranda closed the flat door quietly and respectfully and ran to the office where Gloria immediately rang the police. They were on their way immediately.

Gloria was beside herself with horror. Secretly, she had always been a little in love with Teddy, but she had always known that he was a bastard and a possible rogue. She sighed sadly. She would miss what he had to offer. She telephoned Wilfred who was not at all concerned and just thought 'good riddance to bad rubbish'.

Gloria poured herself, and Miranda, a stiff drink which they both needed.

Inspector Palmer arrived shortly afterwards with Constable George and the paramedics. He was forty-five, brisk and efficient.

"Where's the body?" He wasted no words.

"The flat next door," Gloria sobbed.

"I'll take you," Miranda hurried to show the doctors the way. Gloria and Inspector Palmer followed.

The Inspector inspected the bedroom and the body and then joined Gloria in the lounge. "How were you sure that this man hadn't had a seizure, a fit, or was in a coma?" he asked carefully.

"I was there with Miranda, and she said Teddy was definitely dead," Gloria declared, tears streaming down her face.

"And – is she an authority?" Inspector Palmer asked pointedly.

"She knows a living man from a dead one, that's for sure," Gloria sobbed in despair. "We did our best to wake him up…"

"Well, you did well to telephone us so promptly," Inspector Palmer declared.

Miranda lingered in the doorway.

"Definitely dead," she announced, full of self-importance. "The medics said so."

"And you are?" asked the Inspector.

"Miranda Clark. The cleaner. I know a goner when I see one. I remember my Albert…" she was determined not to be left out of this.

The poor woman probably did not have much excitement in her family life.

"We will have to ask you some questions," Inspector Palmer stated. "It's handy that the Police station is just around the corner."

Gloria murmured yes, but her mind was elsewhere. How could Teddy have died, just like that! Was it an overdose of something?

"It is definitely murder!" stated Miranda positively.

***

The medical examiner confirmed the death. More police arrived and the flat was cordoned off whilst photographs were taken. Miranda, now that she had given her personal details and told them how they had found Teddy, was dismissed. She was not at all happy about it.

Gloria sat in the small lounge as the police went about their business.

Eventually, Inspector Palmer came in to ask her some questions.

"Mr. Jones was on your staff, Mrs. Trent?" he enquired.

"He was my salesman," Gloria said. "He was staying here temporarily until he found a flat of his own. He was good at his job."

"I'm sure he was," Inspector Palmer nodded.

There was a polite knock at the door.

"Come in,"

Constable George entered the room.

"Sir, I've found his laptop," he reported.

"That's a step in the right direction," said Inspector Palmer, pleased.

"Do some more digging around, George. Everything you find will be helpful."

Inspector Palmer turned back to Gloria. "Did Mr. Jones have a family?" he asked.

"He did live with his sister, Emma, until a short time ago," Gloria tried to remember. "I think there was also an aunt."

The medical officer came in, filling in his forms. "Name Teddy Jones, aged about twenty-five. Cause of death? – Not sure yet, could be foul play. There will have to be a post mortem."

"Yes, well, let me know as soon as possible," ordered Inspector Palmer.

"Will do," Medical Officer Stuart Brent closed his notebook. "Ok, if we take the body to the mortuary now?"

"Yes, all the photos have been taken. Seal the room. We'll continue with the investigation of the scene."

"I'll get back to you probably by the end of today," the medical officer promised. "We've not got much on."

"Right," said Inspector Palmer, turning back to Gloria. "You are married, Mrs. Trent," he stated. "Is your husband here?"

"No," Gloria replied. "The property business is my husband's. His name is Wilfred. He had a car crash some time ago and he's housebound."

"You run the business for him?" Inspector Palmer asked. "A capable wife can be such a joy."

Gloria gave him a funny look. "I am Wilfred's second wife, his first did a runner."

Constable George entered with a large plastic bag containing some of Teddy's personal belongings.

"I've found a sort of diary with names and places. Could help quite a lot," he announced. Inspector Palmer was pleased with George. The young lad was doing well.

"Mrs. Trent," Inspector Palmer asked. "How would you describe Mr. Jones?"

Gloria hesitated. She didn't want to get too involved with this. God knows what Wilfred would make of it.

"I think 'a man about town' would be it."

"I see," said Inspector Palmer as he thumbed quickly through the pages. "Hmm, 'Jack the lad', I wouldn't wonder – if this diary is anything to go by."

"I wouldn't know," muttered Gloria.

"Thank you, Mrs. Trent for being so helpful," Inspector Palmer smiled. "You can leave now. I know that your office is next door if we need you, and we probably will."

"Thank you," said Gloria thankfully as she left the flat. With shaking fingers, she lit a cigarette and inhaled deeply.

**

Gloria closed the office early and headed home. Richard was giving Wilfred his supper when she arrived.

"Well, this is a turn up for the books!" said Wilfred. "What happened to Teddy?"

"We don't know yet. All we know is that we found him dead in bed this morning," Gloria said, fighting back tears.

"Who is 'we'?" demanded Wilfred.

"Miranda and me," Gloria choked back a sob. "She'd just arrived to do the cleaning. Teddy had not come in to work. We went to wake him and there he was – dead in bed."

"In my bed!" screamed Wilfred angrily. "Bloody cheek! Are you sure about all this?"

"Yes, it's right enough," Gloria wiped her eyes. "He's as dead as a Dodo."

Richard looked stunned as the dreadful news really sank in. He quickly sat down in the armchair,

"Well, I won't have the trouble of kicking him out of the flat," Wilfred was delighted. "Good news eh, Richard? Really good news."

Gloria went to the drinks cabinet and poured three large whiskies.

"You really shouldn't speak ill of the dead, Wilfred," she muttered.

"Nonsense, woman," Wilfred was in high spirits. "Now let me get on with my supper."

Gloria and Richard exchanged looks as she passed him the whisky.

Wilfred blithely carried on with his supper. "All I can say is that it couldn't have happened to a nicer bloke."

***

Inspector Palmer studied the laptop and diary. From what he could see, there was a lot of interviewing to do. It appeared that Mr. Jones had been quite a player! It was very strange for a young, and seemingly very fit young man to suddenly die in the middle of the night. But first, he would have to go and notify the family. He had found out that there was a sister called Emma Jones living nearby. He was still awaiting the results of the post mortem, and only then could he truly ascertain whether there was foul play involved.

***

Herbert had opened his bookshop and all the publishers had done him proud; the shelves were bursting. They had advanced him all the latest books which were now being reviewed in the press. Local radio and television had heard of the new shop and Herbert had been given radio time on a lunchtime programme. That would be ideal for catching the attention of housewives who made up a big proportion of the book sales. Television was another matter, so the station sent an outside broadcast crew to show the inside and outside of the shop.

The television crew interviewed Herbert separately and let one of their regular announcers do the actual transmission.

Emma had liked the idea of a second-hand section where people could borrow an old book for a small outlay, and return it in exchange for another. This became very popular. Although Emma was the new girl on the block, Herbert was so thrilled to have someone to talk to and share his world with. It gave her such an interest in life and people. Gradually, she was emerging from a nervous, fractious young female into a capable and attractive young lady. The running costs of the shop were minimal, and apart from the first couple of weeks, a little more profit was showing each week.

***

Inspector Palmer and George arrived at Emma's house. They were expecting a tearful meeting with the two relatives upset, and were stunned when it did not happen.

Aunt Clara answered the door. After the formal greetings, they were shown into the front room. Alice was sitting with Emma, enjoying a cup of tea. Aunt Clara was wearing a long woollen dress and the small jet earrings completed a provincial picture. Emma had a plain dress and some colourful ribbons in her hair.

"I regret to tell you that I have some sad news," Palmer began. "Your brother, Miss Jones, was found dead this morning. I am so terribly sorry."

"Oh! Dear," said Emma a little bit matter-of-factly, not really understanding what was being said.

"As far as I am concerned, it's good riddance to bad rubbish!" stated Aunt Clara bluntly.

"Indeed!" said Palmer looking swiftly at George.

"Teddy Jones was a heartless, wicked, scoundrel and his death should be a cause for rejoicing!" said Aunt Clara drawing herself up to full height.

"Surely not, Madam. You are being rather cruel," said Inspector Palmer, taken aback.

"He deserved much more than that. How my poor sister, Rose, could give birth to such a rascal, I don't know. Alice – tell him!"

"You are…?"

"Alice Blake. I live next door."

"If I am not mistaken, you've just bought a hat shop in the High Street."

"Yes," said Alice. "I have a hat shop."

"I only know that because my wife bought a hat from your shop the other day and… I'm sorry, I digress." The Inspector got back on track. "Mr. Jones, was not a popular character?"

"Well, no, not really, you see…" Alice hesitated.

"Shall we proceed, Inspector?" interjected Clara. "I haven't got all day. Emma has a fragile mind, and I am here, not just as a blood relation, but as her carer. Now that we have established that Teddy is dead, is there anything else?"

"Well, we had to first inform you as next of kin," Inspector Palmer declared. "I gather that you didn't exactly get on!"

"That is an understatement," snapped Clara. "I wish I could have killed him myself, and now someone else has done it for me."

"You assume that Mr. Jones was murdered?" Inspector Palmer asked carefully.

"I kicked him out of this house!" Clara stated flatly. "You'd have a seizure if I told you what was going on. Poor Emma."

"Would you like some tea, Inspector?" asked Alice quickly, to change the subject.

"That would be nice," said Inspector Palmer. "George?"

"No, thanks. I'm fine thank you."

"I'll make a pot and you can help yourselves," said Alice. "The kettle has boiled so I won't be long," Alice retreated into the kitchen, anxious to get out of the way.

Emma was extremely nervous and started playing with some beads.

"When's the funeral?" asked Clara.

"Not for a while," the Inspector declared. "The formalities take time, madam. We still have to ascertain the cause of death."

"I always said he would end up badly," declared Clara. "Ha! Drink, drugs, women, gambling – he did the lot!"

"You seem to be well informed, madam."

"You can ask anyone that knew him!" stated Clara.

"He did have some good points," said Emma quietly.

"You'd have a difficult job finding them!" retorted Clara.

"Did you like your brother, Emma?" asked Inspector Palmer gently.

She looked at him, but kept quiet.

"Really, Inspector, that's not a fair question," barked Clara. "Let's say the poor child didn't understand him, thank God!"

There was a long silence broken by the distant rattle of tea cups as Alice made her way from the kitchen.

"Here I am," Alice said as she came in. "Now Inspector, do you take sugar?"

"Only when I have to," Inspector Palmer said.

"Not good for the brain, Inspector," she said lightly as she gave him a cup.

"I realise this is a difficult time for you," the Inspector said. "When would you like to answer some questions?"

"About what?" asked Clara, rising to get her cup.

"I was talking to Emma if you don't mind," said Palmer.

"Emma takes time to think," Clara said sharply.

"I have to go to the shop," Emma mumbled.

"Shop?"

"Yes, I have a shop and it's full of books," Emma said hesitantly.

"Emma has a share in the new book shop in town, Inspector and we are due there this very hour, if you don't mind!" Clara rattled her teaspoon in the cup impatiently.

"Well, perhaps that will be all for now," Inspector Palmer took the hint and finished his tea quickly. "I will have to come and speak to you again when we know more. I am sorry for your loss."

"Well, we certainly are not!" Clara declared. "I wish you good day, Inspector Palmer, and whatever your name is."

"Constable George, Madam."

"Good lord, it speaks! Enough!" said Clara as she waved them out of the room.

"Before we go, I think I should make myself clear," Inspector Palmer stated seriously, eyeing Clara severely. "I have a job to do. I will interview as I choose. Teddy Jones has died in suspicious circumstances and, in English law, you are obliged to answer all the questions that I may think necessary. I will be back to interrogate you further. Until then, I wish you good day."

Inspector Palmer and Constable George left the room, leaving Clara, Emma and Alice speechless.

As they left, Inspector Palmer noticed a shadowy figure lurking across the street.

***

Back at the Police Station, Constable George was looking through Teddy's notebook diary, and laptop.

"I've got a feeling that there was more to Teddy Jones' salesmanship where Gloria Trent was concerned. She was a bit of alright, don't you think?"

"Good looking woman," commented Inspector Palmer, "and I think the deceased was one for the ladies, too."

"Did you notice – he was hung like a donkey!" said Constable George.

"As I said, there's more to this than meets the eye," said Palmer with a cough, giving George a sharp look.

"I mean, I know many who would like to have half of what he had," said the Constable jealously.

Inspector Palmer enjoyed his job. He had been an only child and lived a bachelor's life. He looked after his ageing mother in a semi-detached house and women never seemed to enter his orbit.

Constable George, on the other hand, was very interested in the opposite sex. He had lost his virginity when he was fifteen and experience was his middle name. His latest squeeze was a policewoman called Shirley, who obliged once in a while. She was a little precious and always considered that opening her legs was doing one a favour!"

Chapter Twelve

Emma had taken Teddy's death very well, and it was such a consolation that she had started work at the bookshop. She had much to do to help Herbert who was in seventh heaven with his new empire. He took interest in his customers, which he felt was essential when one started a new business. He found that a little chat when they purchased a book could work wonders. Emma was quickly sorting out books and authors and getting them onto the correct shelves. Her white blouse and black skirt looked ideal for her new role. Herbert had never had such a friend.

***

Inspector Palmer had Wilfred on his interrogation list and a visit was imminent.

Constable George arranged Palmer's interview for ten the following morning.

Wilfred had dressed for the occasion and wore his green blazer plus grey slacks. Richard was in attendance as always, and was more casually dressed. The doorbell rang promptly and Richard answered the door. After introducing themselves, the questions began.

"We have met your wife, Gloria, Mr. Trent and it was she that found the body. You must have known Teddy Jones fairly well. After all, you did employ him," said Palmer.

"Yes," said Wilfred, "but that was Gloria's doing. Personally, I loathed the man. I have often thought I'd like to kill him, but it seems someone has saved me the job."

"How did you come across Mr. Jones?"

"My wife advertised for a salesman and Teddy Jones applied," answered Wilfred. "Oh, and may I introduce you to Richard, my live-in carer and companion. He knew Teddy better than I."

"Good morning," said Inspector Palmer looking Richard over. "So you knew Teddy Jones?"

"We met a few times," Richard tried to sound casual, "but I didn't really know him very well."

"Would you say he was very active in the sex department?" the inspector asked.

"Oh yes," Wilfred interrupted. "From what I've heard, he would service anyone, man, woman, or donkey."

Inspector Palmer gave Constable George a knowing look.

"That's rather a broad statement, sir, if I may say so."

Wilfred eased himself in his chair. "It sums up his character, and I honestly couldn't be more pleased that he has kicked the bucket."

Inspector Palmer turned to Richard. "Would you go along with that, sir?"

Richard blushed. "As I said, I didn't know him that well. I only met him when I delivered Wilfred's letters to the office." He paused. "When will the funeral be, Inspector?"

Wilfred frowned, "A funeral! I hope not! Chuck him in a ditch, I would say!"

Inspector Palmer was at a loss for words. "Well, I think that is all, gentlemen," he declared awkwardly. "I appreciate your time."

With that, Inspector Palmer and Constable George withdrew, leaving Wilfred to assess the visit with Richard.

***

Clara was determined to protect Emma at all costs. She knew what snakes the press could be – anything for a story, anything for the nitty gritty. After all, a little extra in the pay packet was always welcome for a hack reporter.

Clara was secretly astonished at the change in Emma. It was quite extraordinary!

Life could be unbelievable at times, and a rosebud could suddenly develop into a bloom. She was pleased and Alice thanked her God for the transformation.

Alice was pleased that the vicar, Aubrey, liked Emma. Every new member in his flock was ammunition to the vicar in the next parish who considered himself and the members in his parish, the crème de la crème. Even vicars played the popularity game. Aubrey caressed the cross that he displayed proudly on his chest, and told himself secretly that miracles could happen.

***

The next name that Palmer and George came across in the book was Fay.

They contacted the supermarket as this was their only contact and arranged an interview. The manager, a Mr. Felton, didn't really approve of the situation, as he felt that the police station would have been a more suitable place for an interrogation. Fay didn't want to lose money over it and asked for it to be held at the supermarket in the staff rest room.

Inspector Palmer was brief and to the point. "I believe you knew Teddy Jones?"

"Yes," Fay answered, not knowing where this was leading.

"He was a customer here?" the Inspector asked.

"Yes," she said quietly.

"Do you mind if I ask you a personal question?"

"No, sir," Fay shifted uncomfortably in her seat.

"Did you have a sexual relationship with Mr. Jones?"

Fay was a little stunned. That was a little near the knuckle. What would her mother say?

"Yes, once or twice!" she admitted.

Constable George had been diligently writing in his notepad. "How old are you, Miss?" he asked.

"Eighteen and a half!" Fay whispered.

The words had scarcely left her lips when the door burst open and Daisy entered. Inspector Palmer was not amused by the interruption.

"Madam, this is a private interview," he declared frostily.

Daisy pulled herself up to her full height. "That may be, but I am Fay's mother, and I want to know what is going on!" She gave the Inspector a look that would have silenced a revolution. Inspector Palmer could see that this was going to be a trickier situation than he had anticipated. This woman was a firecracker.

"I think we had better continue this interview at the station, if you don't mind, Miss," he declared.

Daisy snorted angrily. "But I do mind!"

Inspector Palmer motioned to Constable George.

"Perhaps you would both come with me. I have a car outside."

"I am not going anywhere until I know what this is all about!" shrieked Daisy.

"Mrs and Miss Bennett, I'm sorry to tell you that Mr. Teddy Jones has been found dead!" Inspector Palmer declared.

"No!" Fay sat down, stunned.

"Oh! Really?" Daisy looked pleased.

"Now, ladies, we will continue this down at the station," ordered Palmer. Reluctantly, Daisy and Fay were ushered out of the supermarket and into the waiting police car.

***

The day of the first transmission of the commercial arrived and it was shown twenty-four times in twenty-four hours. The butterfly motif and the soap it illustrated looked immense. Frazer looked great with his toned physique and, if you didn't rave about the soap, you had an eyeful of Mr. Lloyd!

Emma arrived home about six and Alice was in a state of excitement.

"Emma, your commercial has been on all day, and it looks fabulous. I have telephoned Aunt Clara, and she is very pleased." The two women were thrilled that something wonderful was happening, and it could mean many gold pieces for Emma.

"Has it been on all day?" asked Emma hardly concealing her excitement.

"Practically, and you know that every time it is shown, you get a tiny piece of the cake!"

"Does Frazer look wonderful?" asked Emma.

Alice smiled. She was so pleased with Emma's new found interest in everything. "Yes. He is every housewife's dream, I reckon, and what it does for Butterfly soap is something again. I'm going out to buy some this afternoon."

The telephone rang and Alice answered.

"It's Frazer, Emma."

Alice had never been so excited. In her mundane life, nothing like this had ever happened before. Emma grabbed the phone, and the sun beamed through the windows.

Alice was going shopping. She might buy two bars of Butterfly soap that afternoon!

***

At the police station, Daisy was getting quite heated. Fay asked her mother to be quiet, but to no avail.

"He seduced my daughter, and she's under age. I want compensation!"

"Your daughter told us she was eighteen and a half," said George referring to his notepad.

"You silly bitch!" Daisy swore. "You never know when to keep your mouth shut. She's sixteen next week! That bastard, I would kill him, if I could get my hands on him!"

"You've missed the boat there, I'm afraid," said Inspector Palmer grimly. Daisy sat down. This was really a turn up for the books and she could see her demands for cash had suddenly gone out of the window. Fay wiped away a tear.

"Now look what you've done to my daughter! She's upset! Really Inspector you should know better!"

Inspector Palmer didn't know what to make of this distraught woman.

"Mrs. Bennett, did you meet Teddy Jones?" he asked.

"Yes, I had a confrontation with him. He assaulted my Fay!"

Constable George surreptitiously signalled to the Inspector. Inspector Palmer stood up quickly.

"If you'll excuse us for a moment," he said. "We won't be very long."

Inspector Palmer and Constable George left the room.

"I've seen her before, on the laptop," announced the Constable. "There are some very explicit photos of her on there!"

"We'd better look into this!"

Ten minutes later, they re-entered the interviewing room with the laptop.

"I think you knew Teddy Jones a little better than you let on, Mrs. Bennett," Inspector Palmer declared grimly.

"What do you mean?" exclaimed Daisy indignantly. Fay dried her eyes and looked puzzled.

Constable George placed the laptop in front of Daisy, and there was one of the photos Teddy had taken of her when he had drugged her when she visited him.

"You seem to have your mouth full in that one," commented Constable George rudely.

"Fuck!" said Daisy.

"I think we have a little explaining to do, Mrs Bennett," Inspector Palmer stated seriously.

***

The following day, Inspector Palmer and Constable George arrived at Herbert's new bookshop. Emma had already told Herbert the news of Teddy's demise. The only time Herbert had met Teddy was when he had paid him forty pounds to meet Emma.

Herbert shook with nerves as he relayed the whole affair to the policemen. Now they understood why Clara had thrown Teddy out of the house.

Constable George scribbled everything down in his notepad.

"Quite a character this Teddy Jones," he commented.

***

Inspector Palmer and Constable George followed up by visiting the club called 'Georgina's'. The receptionist Rupert panicked somewhat with the arrival of the police. "Can I help you, sir?" He emphasised 'sir' to try and ingratiate himself.

"I believe you have a member called Teddy Jones at the club," Inspector Palmer began.

"Do we? I will have to check," Rupert tried to look super-efficient. He opened the large membership book on the desk, and rattled through a few pages.

"Oh, yes. Mr. Jones was here two weeks ago," said Rupert triumphantly.

The smile left his face when Inspector George asked him for his name.

"I'm Rupert Gordon. I've worked here for three years." Constable George diligently wrote it all down in his pad. Inspector Palmer looked at the many leaflets on display, and helped himself to some.

"It's a private members club," added Rupert.

"Who owns the club?"

Rupert hesitated for a moment not knowing quite what to say.

"I'm waiting," prodded Constable George.

"Georgina, Georgina Ryan."

"Miss or Mrs?" asked George.

"That is a difficult question Inspector. He's a transvestite," said Rupert blushing.

"Oh! Really! Who did Teddy Jones meet here at the club?" asked Inspector Palmer, joining the fray.

"Um..." Rupert did not know what to say.

"I take it that special services were on offer," the Inspector stated drily.

Rupert was getting redder by the minute. "He was here three times that I know of. We do sometimes provide escorts."

"And he was an escort?"

"I don't know. I think so..." stuttered Rupert.

"Is Georgina Ryan in?" Inspector Palmer asked politely.

"I'll check," said Rupert. "She may be with a client."

"Then, I think you ought to interrupt her," said Inspector Palmer firmly, leaning on Rupert's desk. Rupert scuttled off to find Georgina.

"I think it's a knocking shop, George," said Inspector Palmer. "Let's take a look."

They entered the club. There were a few clients in the bar area, who all seemed a little intimidated that they were there. Obviously they were not there just for a drink.

"One thing you must say about this job, George," commented the Inspector. "It's never dull!"

It was all a little seedy in the light of day, but then, so was Teddy Jones.

There were several payments of one hundred pounds in Teddy's diary, all under the name Georgina. This had to be investigated. Suddenly, there was a deep voice behind them.

"Well, gentlemen, what can I do for you?" She stood there in a very short, skimpy, sequined dress and a ton of make-up.

"Inspector Palmer and Constable George. We're here on official business."

They flashed their credentials, and Georgina took them through to the small bar. Sitting at the bar was a lady wearing a short cocktail dress sipping a martini. It was Rita.

"So how can I help you?" purred Georgina.

"I believe you know Teddy Jones," said Inspector Palmer sitting at a small round table.

"Yes, he was one of our members," Georgina answered smoothly.

"He was a whore!" gurgled Rita into her Martini.

Georgina tried to silence the drunken Rita, but to no avail.

"The fucker didn't oblige and pissed off. I paid good money!"

"Take no notice gentlemen," Georgina interrupted quickly. "Rita has had one too many. I haven't seen Teddy for about three weeks. What's he done?"

"I'm afraid that Teddy Jones has been found dead," said George.

"Good!" said Rita raising her glass.

Georgina was stunned. "When…where?"

"Last night in his flat,"

"How did he die? Was he? You know what I mean!"

"We will know more when the autopsy is done," said the Inspector.

"Well, he was an insulting bastard, and probably deserved it," snarled Rita.

"So – Teddy was engaged as a male escort," declared the Inspector.

"He was engaged by me to entertain my guests," said Georgina cautiously. "Customer care, Inspector."

"And you haven't seen him for three weeks," said George filling in his notepad as usual.

"That's right," said Georgina.

"Good riddance to bad rubbish," said Rita nearly falling off her perch.

"Very well," the Inspector got up to go. "That will be all for now, er… Miss er… Ryan. We will probably be back for more questions later."

Inspector Palmer and Constable George left the bar. Georgina went behind the bar and poured herself a very large gin.

Chapter Thirteen

Aunt Clara was making herself a cup of tea when Alice popped in.

"Any news, Clara?" she asked.

"No. Nothing," declared Clara. "All this carry on about Teddy – as if it matters. He has only got what he deserved, and this is not a situation that I want to be associated with."

"Emma's coping with it very well," Alice commented.

"She'll be back from the shop soon," Clara smiled. "I must say, she seems like a new woman."

"What happens next?" Alice asked.

"I suppose we'll have to organise the funeral," Clara frowned. "I hope he's insured. It's the sort of thing my sister would have covered."

***

The Butterfly Soap commercial was shown at least ten times a day.

They had done an excellent job on Emma's butterfly, which looked resplendent with its coat of many colours. Frazer was in seventh heaven. He had already had some casting agents on the telephone – they could smell success like a fox trails a rabbit.

Two more commercial auditions had been arranged. He had, several seasons ago, given the casting director a quick screwing. He remembered her vividly, with her panting and feverish desire for more.

At the time, he had been a mere twenty-three, and she was a well upholstered forty-two. Rome wasn't built in a day, but that little frolic had paid dividends for several months until he had gone out of fashion. He was reading the morning paper when he came across the report of Teddy's death.

He had often wished that he could get at Teddy for using Emma in such a deplorable way. He thought back to the day that he had visited Emma. He recalled her little face, so fragile and frightened.

He had forgotten all about his desire for sex and, instead, had given her kisses she would treasure always. His visit was a one off. His girlfriend, Julia, had left him for a rich jeweller who offered ravishing on a spectacular scale. That day, he had been randy – but now he despised himself for even considering Emma's availability. Everyone had their off day, and that had been his. Now, he would never get even with Teddy Jones, who had now got his just desserts. However, he would be certain to make it up to Emma.

He telephoned Emma immediately to make sure that she was alright and she was. He had so much to thank her for, and also Sam, who had instigated the whole butterfly experience. Frazer made a date and he took Emma out to dinner and it was a delight. At last he could do something for the girl, and her excitement of the whole affair was something to cherish and remember. He found young Emma a delightful companion, but romance was not on the cards. Nevertheless, affection was priceless and he was to bask in her adoration for many years to come.

***

Emma's world was changing so rapidly that she had a job catching up with it. Looking back at the interlude fashioned by Teddy, wonderful things had come out of the experiment. She had met Sam whom she adored and helped her discover her amazing talent for design. Frazer had become a great friend, and her friend, Herbert, now had a shop. She retained some feelings for her brother; after all, she thought, nobody is perfect.

Sam had come to worship Emma, and she slowly realised that she had fallen in love with the young man. The pairing couldn't have been more right. It was romantic and would prove to be a wonderful love affair that would have excited even Hollywood.

***

Wilfred was relieved and pleased that Teddy Jones had gone. He had never trusted him and certainly, if he had had his way, would never have employed him. Gloria had won the day on that one.

If Wilfred had been psychic, he would have known that Richard had also enjoyed Teddy's fruits. Richard had enjoyed his sexual scene with Teddy and had found it thrilling as well as very satisfying. He was very sad that he couldn't enjoy Teddy's company any more. Now, he had Abigail to contend with, and it didn't really suit him at all. Wilfred was also getting jealous of his absences, when he had to go and service Abigail.

***

Gloria was in the office when a mature woman arrived. Her name was Cynthia Rayburn. She was forty-five going on fifty. She wore a beautiful tailored suit which she accessorised with a stunning pearl necklace and matching earrings.

"You are Gloria Trent?" she enquired, rather pompously.

"I was when I last looked," Gloria replied with a smile.

"I believe you employ a certain Teddy Jones," the woman began.

"Well, I was engaged to Mr. Jones and loaned him five thousand pounds to set up a project he had in mind."

"Really?" Gloria was intrigued. "That was courageous of you."

"But he seems to have disappeared! Vanished!" the woman exclaimed angrily.

"A fiancé who is not where he should be is always trying, especially where finance is concerned."

"I'm sorry," Gloria said. "I didn't get your name."

"Cynthia Rayburn," the woman declared, furiously spitting the words out.

"Where is the cad? I've a good mind to cancel the engagement. I'll kill the bugger when I get hold of him."

Gloria smiled secretly to herself. The poor cow had arrived too late.

The fiancé had gone and so had her five grand.

"Would you be more worried about your money, or your engagement?" Gloria inquired carefully.

"Money doesn't matter!" Cynthia Rayburn waved her hand dismissively.

"Daddy is very rich so I don't worry about money. Teddy is a bad boy, but he does have some very good things to recommend him."

Cynthia had definitely reached the station but too late. The train had gone!

"I'm afraid you are a little late in this case," Gloria stated. "Teddy Jones has just been found dead!"

"You must be joking!" Cynthia exclaimed.

"I can assure you, I'm not," Gloria declared.

Cynthia asked the usual questions, when, where, how, could he have been murdered. She looked dismayed and Gloria asked her if she wanted a glass of water which she declined.

Cynthia looked at Gloria, sizing her up. This dame was as cool as a cucumber. Cynthia had known that Teddy hadn't really been marriage material, but he had helped her pass the time in a dull season, and she crossed her legs remembering what he had to offer.

"I don't want anything said about my association with Teddy," Cynthia declared flatly.

"Miss Rayburn," Gloria said firmly. "I employed Teddy Jones and any publicity generated from this unfortunate affair is up to the police. They have already been here asking questions."

"Well, keep me out of this," ordered Cynthia. "Only Daddy knew of my engagement to Teddy. It could easily be lost in the passage of time."

"I'm not too sure," Gloria looked doubtful. "If I don't tell Inspector Palmer, someone else is bound to."

Cynthia quickly opened her capacious handbag and produced a chequebook.

"I could make it worth your while," she said.

"I don't know. This needs to be thought out," said Gloria, shaking her head. She did not trust Miss Rayburn. She was too sure of herself.

Had she really not known that Teddy was dead, and was this visit all a facade? If she wrote a cheque, then she would be able to trace it, and implicate her if she had to.

***

The day was cloudy, the cemetery sombre. A few flowers were drooping either from lack of moisture or lack of affection for Teddy Jones. The bell tolled slowly as the coffin was taken into the church.

Aunt Clara wore her black straw hat from Alice's collection. She thought he didn't really deserve it, but it gave it an outing. Emma was quiet. She wore her grey woollen dress and a black raincoat. She couldn't quite understand Teddy's death. They said that they thought that, somehow, he might have misjudged the drugs he was taking.

Did he take them himself or did someone else give them to him? There were only a few mourners. Abigail, Cynthia, Wendy and Gloria all wore black. Richard sat with them with Fay Bennet across the aisle.

Sam and Frazer were there to support Emma, and Glenn was there to support Aubrey the priest. Inspector Palmer and Constable George sat at the back of the church. The priest's address was short. After all, what could you say about Teddy Jones except ask for forgiveness.

Aunt Clara had chosen some suitable hymns which she had chosen in memory of her sister Rose. Emma held back the tears, comforted by Sam, who held her hand. Aunt Clara sat erect, desperate to dismiss any form of affection or forgiveness. Suddenly, the church door creaked open and Daisy Bennet swept down the aisle to her daughter.

"Fay! What are you doing!" she hissed angrily. "How you have the nerve to sit there, I will never know!" With that, Daisy quietly withdrew to a pew at the rear of the church.

Inspector Palmer smiled at George. He had done his homework well and the post mortem had clearly shown that an overdose of drugs had taken the life of Teddy Jones.

"Death by misadventure," Inspector Palmer muttered in disappointment. "I was sure we had a murder."

George nodded but didn't jot it down.

The ceremony was done, and the undertaker took over and the coffin was taken slowly out of the church, followed by the few mourners.

Aunt Clara took Emma's hand and Sam followed behind. Emma was glad the service was over, and as she left the church, she noticed the man in black under a low hanging yew tree. He was smiling. Had she seen him before? What did it all mean?

The End